THE

KATJA PERAT

THE MASOCHIST

Translated from the Slovenian by
Michael Biggins

istrosbooks

First published in 2020 by **Istros Books**
(in collaboration with Beletrina Academic Press)
London, United Kingdom
www.istrosbooks.com

Originally published in Slovene in 2018 as *Mazohistka*
by Beletrina Academic Press, 2007

Translation © Michael Biggins, 2020

Cover design and typesetting: Davor Pukljak, www.frontispis.hr

ISBN: 978-1-912545-17-9

This Book is part of the EU co-funded project *"Reading the Heart of Europe"*
in partnership with Beletrina Academic Press | www.beletrina.si

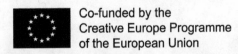

Co-funded by the
Creative Europe Programme
of the European Union

The European Commission support for the production of this publication does not constitute an endorsement
of the contents which reflects the views only of the authors, and the Commission cannot be held responsible
for any use which may be made of the information contained therein.

If the facts indicate otherwise, then too bad for the facts.

1

"You don't look anything like him," the innkeeper said, his eyes narrowing in disbelief. His German was harsh, but impeccable. He tried his utmost to keep others from accusing him of not trying his utmost. Even his lodgings, circumstances aside, testified to his pedantry. It was a hole in the wall three doors down from the Armenian Orthodox church, in the centre of town (although, truth to tell, was anything in Lemberg really downtown), squeezed in between the neighbouring buildings and the street, upholstered with drunks, and yet every tablecloth, every drinking glass was neatly arranged in its place, as if in a show-room. He had to be trying his utmost – the innkeeper – to keep order in this place, with nobody looking, with everything constantly straining towards chaos.

"You don't look a thing like him." And to be perfectly honest, I didn't. I looked much more like this stranger of an innkeeper, if only with respect to our hair colour, than I looked like Leopold. It would have been quite the comedy if it actually turned out that this man was my father.

His tone of voice hinted that I should take the emphasis on the difference as a compliment, although there was no warmth to accompany it. The determination with which he sustained the conversation surprised me a bit; particularly because it was obvious it gave him no pleasure. He asked his questions – where I was from, where I was going – questions that, asked in a different way, might have seemed frivolous, but which his inborn sense of annoyance made seem like an interrogation. He wasn't exactly what you'd call the salt of the earth, this innkeeper. He was cold and practical, not effusive. At the mention of my surname he immediately recalled the old chief of police, a good man, he said, and only then recollected that the police chief had a son, who apparently had become a writer, he said.

"With quite a vivid imagination, I've heard tell," he said as he wiped a glass dry. "Imagining that you're being whipped by women in furs, that's a fantasy that only somebody who's never been whipped can indulge. You don't look a thing like him."

What he really meant to say was that Leopold von Sacher-Masoch was a disgusting human being, but you somehow seem likeable. "Are you sure you're his daughter?"

Although, strictly speaking, it wasn't the truth, Leopold would gladly tell anyone who had a moment to spare the story of his wild child.

"This is Nada, my wild child," he would say and repeat until it finally stuck and everyone who knew him also knew that he had adopted and was raising a wild child. Considering the fact that he found me when I was barely a day old, there hadn't been even the slightest chance that I'd grown up in a cage kept by some madman or been raised by Carpathian mountain men, or by wolves, but why bother with facts when fiction is so much more useful?

Judging from the way Leopold peddled the story of my birth, you could tell that it would have best served his interests if I'd had no human parents at all. He also liked to emphasize that, no, he really wasn't my father, as though he couldn't imagine that the girl who placed all her trust and all the love of her childhood in him would ever take that as the most fundamental, the most unconditional rejection of all. Yes, I suppose he loved me, but his love could really be useless.

How unfair, I often thought after Anna died, that the woman for whom my birth and the pregnancy preceding it, and possibly even the love that preceded the pregnancy had been real concerns – that that woman never found her way into Leopold's stories, despite the fact that Leopold always liked to say that women, not men, were the ones who should be entrusted with history.

I know. No child witnesses her own birth, but there was something about the way Leopold cast the story of my birth as a mystery that made me feel from early on that I knew less about myself than others did. He had two contradictory theories, both of them fantastic, both of them beautiful, but neither of them true. According to the first theory I'd grown up out of the earth. According to the second I'd been dropped from the sky.

The first went something like this: on Christmas Day 1874 Leopold disappeared without a trace. Later it turned out that after a years-long absence he paid a short visit to Lemberg. As befits a deep thinker and cosmopolitan who wants to contemplate life, one afternoon he set out on a walk through the woods, where atop a heap of broken branches and new-fallen snow he discovered a basket. And wherever there's a basket, so the fairy tales go, there must be a child. Alive, by some miracle.

It was so easy to share in his joy. Leopold was too much of an enthusiast and his sense of reality too weak for him to pause to entertain second thoughts. He removed the cloth that covered the basket (in his telling the cloth was chequered, as per tradition) and beheld my eyes (in his telling as traditionally dark as the night sky over the Carpathians – Leopold was so fond of exaggerating). As far as Leopold was concerned, there wasn't a doubt. And thus his wild child project was born scarcely a day later, I'd wager, than me. It was clear to him: the girl that he'd found in the forest was no mere girl. She was the essence of the Slavonic soul, and how could she not be, when, like every idea worth its name, she'd sprouted straight out of the earth of her homeland. Perhaps that's why he was fond of repeating that, no, he wasn't my father (but that's incredible, she's the spitting image of you, someone would invariably say, even though it wasn't true), because he bore the mark of guilt. His blood was the blood of the oppressor, while I had to remain pure. I had to at least retain the potential, if only I chose (and oh, how he tried to get me to choose), to play my historical role. It was never a hundred per cent clear what that role was supposed to be, what were its practical aspects, or with what political means I was supposed to perform it, but the goal, as hazy as it was, was clear from the start: I'd been born to wipe out inequities and set wrongs to right. Although he was generally fond of singing paeans of praise to his homeland's ethnic diversity, he often hinted that I could become the Liberté of the Slavs. Though if I insisted, I could of course make do with less, but what a shame, what a terrible shame that would be, considering everything that had been vouchsafed me as a birthright.

The second story began like the first, but instead of historical it assumed metaphysical dimensions. Leopold had vanished in the dead of night, stumbling off in a delirium to discover his roots. Lemberg, the forest and the child in the basket were unchanging props. But this time the child, a red-haired girl, didn't sprout from the earth, but fell to earth like a shooting star in the frigid winter night, like a fallen angel sent to enchant all the mortals it might encounter and rule over their hearts. As I've mentioned, Leopold loved extremes.

I realized that my birth was a kind of literature for him. I was like Athena, born straight out of his head. Like other mythological creatures, I'd been created to presage something more significant than myself. But the child refuses to presage anything. The child wants to be significant in its own right.

You have to know this: Leopold adored cats. Wherever he went, he always brought a cat back with him that was at least as cute as it was abandoned – and each time it was impossible to say which quality weighed more for him, the cuteness or the abandonment. It wasn't long before I realized that I occupied a similar niche in his life. I was a stray orange tabby that drew his attention and got itself taken home, so that he could distract himself with it for a minute or two when he didn't have anything more important to do.

So in short, no, I wasn't *really* Leopold's daughter. Despite that, I wanted to protect him from the avalanche of scorn that the innkeeper's heedless mention of Leopold's masochism threatened, the thoughtless cruelty of the little people whose cause he took up so often, but who saw in him little more than an unctuous aristocrat who could afford the luxury of a perverse imagination, because reality treated him with kid gloves and spared him any real concerns. It was all too easy for me to imagine my mother, a peasant, an actress, a Gypsy, or whatever she was, a pissed-off woman shoving her way through the saloon door and sitting down at the bar, ordering, tossing her drink back, and seeing me the way that innkeeper saw Leopold. As though everything that haunts me is meaningless, hollow, made up. If I knew how to say something to protect Leopold from ridicule, I'd be protecting myself, too, in a way. But I couldn't. He was too angry, the innkeeper was, to leave any room for compassion. It was small comfort to me that I wasn't the object of his rage. If not physically, then at least spiritually Leopold and I were too much alike for me not to feel personally offended by anyone who offended him.

I disappeared from Vienna with the same melodramatic flair that he did. As if to say, "There, now that I'm gone, I dare you to fathom the extent of your loss." And, like him, I also couldn't quite figure out how to soften the disappointment brought about by the chasm separating my expectations from reality. I don't know exactly what I was hoping for from Lemberg when I got on the train. That it would reveal itself to me as the home I'd never had? Offer me answers to the questions I'd never been able to ask those nearest to me without making them fidget? A fairy tale in which crystalline snow crunches under the runners of a sleigh festooned with bells? Inner tranquillity? Whatever I'd hoped for, what I got were the inn-keeper's sneering face, some overcooked dumplings, and the gaunt reality of a province where from behind their shutters the people kept zealous watch on each other, but especially on me, who had no business being there, anyway.

Leopold had to work very hard to attribute everything he adored, but refused to be responsible for, to this land. And if it had only been a matter of the land, which, sworn to silence, was by definition incapable of defending itself, things might have worked out. But with the land came people. And those people would have preferred to be able to speak for themselves than have a man speak for them who had squandered his whole fortune buying countless fur coats for his many lovers.

As the innkeeper might have said, you know, I think I prefer the monarchy as it is to pan-Slavism with an Austrian face. I mean, come on, what does that even mean?

It was amusing to watch him speak with great passion and at length about Leopold, despite the fact that he must have been consti-tutionally predisposed to feel nothing but revulsion for him, because here at least was someone whose flaws could be the measure of his own infallibility. Leopold's political philosophy was sheer twaddle, an invention of his perverted mind, a game that rich people play when they're bored. His, however, was born of necessity, which lent it power and gravitas. Justified by the life he'd been forced to live. His faith in himself made me uncomfortable, but, to be perfectly honest, more than anything else I envied him. His certainty, solidity, linearity. His groundedness. No wonder, then, that he took to me, considering that my whole being affirmed his personal choices.

It was obvious: if I had travelled to the edge of the world to witness a revelation, I'd travelled in vain. But we all know I wasn't after a revelation. Like Leopold, I'd also come here to escape responsibility.

"Absolutely positive," I said to the innkeeper. "I swear I'm his daughter."

He squinted and nodded sceptically.

"That's strange," he said. "You don't look a thing like him."

"My husband recently shot and killed my lover," I said. Let me repeat: it was personality, not facial features, that made me Leopold's daughter.

"I'm listening," he said, and set down a glass of vodka in front of me.

Maybe I was wrong. Maybe, in spite of everything, he still had some room for compassion. Or maybe it was just curiosity. Sometimes it can be hard to tell them apart.

2 It would be wrong to say that Maximilian was ugly. Whenever I looked at him from a distance, whenever he was shuffling his papers or reading the newspaper with just enough light, I could sometimes convince myself that all the people who insisted he really was handsome were right. And yet later, when I was reading *Anna Karenina*, I knew that Tolstoy had made a mistake. It wasn't possible for Anna to notice only later how big her husband's ears were. She had to have known that from the very start, and it just took her that long to admit it. Like me when Maximilian slurped his food, she must have looked away and tried to convince herself that whatever was bothering her was inconsequential and would, with time, dissipate all by itself.

It would also be wrong to say that he didn't love me. Like Leopold, he also adored the story of the wild child. And my red hair. And my stupid name. Nadezhda, "Hope", what a mean joke. Hope, Leopold liked to say, there's hope hidden in your name. And, funny as it may seem, he was right in a way. Hope was hidden in my name – hope that one day somebody would know how to pronounce it correctly. That one day somebody wouldn't have to ask me what it was twice, only to fall politely silent after asking the third time. Hope that one day it would just slide past unnoticed, without some society lady remarking with feigned insouciance that that was her maidservant's name. Maximilian liked anything that seemed exotic, especially if it wasn't really foreign and didn't needlessly vex him with some enigma, which made me, with my name, red hair and pedigree a natural choice for him. Without any doubt, that was itself a form of love in its own right. And, of course, it's entirely possible that each time I fixated on my sense of anxiety that he didn't love me or, at least, didn't love me enough, I was trying to avoid dealing with the fact that it was actually me who was coming up short on the love.

I met him in Lindheim, the town where I learned to hate Leopold, and I don't exclude the possibility that that hatred was precisely the thing that forced me to redirect what I had once felt for Leopold onto some other person.

We moved to Lindheim, the dullest of all dull German towns, because Leopold decided that in his old age he was going to see yet again if love didn't exist after all, and after divorcing Wanda, with whom he had lived until then, he got remarried to Hulda, his secretary and translator.

Overnight one life replaced the other and then settled in with us for a while. Hulda's house became our home, as did Lindheim, even though everything about it was repulsive. Though this wasn't my first time living in a small town, in Lindheim I lived a small-town life for the first time, governed as it was by the passage from meal to meal, with brief intervals for study, errands and the occasional walk. My hatred was unfair to Lindheim, no doubt, but even so the injustice of it didn't diminish its force. I hated it because I hated Hulda and because it had been forced on me as a result of Leopold's rashness.

To this day I don't know whether Leopold left Wanda or if it was really the other way around and Wanda left Leopold, but even then I knew that their divorce wasn't going to amount to anything more than a minor edit to his biography, while it could deprive her of any chance of a normal life. Even though she was probably never truly happy with Leopold and she devoted most of her energy to keeping him financially and emotionally above water, as though her own well-being was a matter of secondary importance to her, she was settled with him, and without him the world had no fixed point of reference.

Poor Wanda, I thought as I watched her efforts to carve out a right to her own account of their divorce. And how little good it did her – with what cruel spontaneity everyone showed their preference for Leopold. With what cruel spontaneity even I showed my preference for him, fully aware of how unjust that was, even when I hated him most. How greedily I sought his attention and recognition, how happy I was when he decided after the divorce to take me with him to Lindheim. Leopold was crazy, of course: maniacal, neurasthenic, overwrought. Everyone agreed about that. But he was like a child who simply can't be called to account. Wanda, on the other hand, now she was calculating, chasing after him on account of his title, a slut, a furious bitch who couldn't muster enough humility and grace to endure her lot as a divorced woman in silence. Even in my childish compassion there was something shallow, like an inchoate fear that if I didn't grow up right, there might be something like that in store for me, a sense of unease at the thought that while love might still be there in the morning, when you tried to reach for it in the evening, there would be nothing but lifeless indifference left on your bedside table. My compassion was so shallow that you could scarcely call it compassion. I felt as though everything that was happening was happening first and foremost to me. And just as though I'd been abandoned myself, the thought of how quickly Wanda had been replaced and how vulgar her successor was plunged me into despair.

Although Hulda was my parent about as much as Wanda had been, I always thought of her as a stepmother and suspiciously waited for the day when she was going to offer me a poisoned apple or hire some hunter to track me down and serve up my lungs and liver as edible proof of my demise. While it was no surprise that she couldn't look on the remains of Leopold's former life with anything approaching compassion, what was striking was that any under-standing of it at all seemed to be beyond her grasp, and the fact that amongst the remains there were children who bore no responsibility, much less guilt for all that wasn't the least bit an obstacle to her in exercising her spite. She was cold and cruel with a coldness and cruelty that were no masquerade, no disguise that a person can put on and take off, as if putting on and taking off a fur coat. They were real, profane, and trite. When Sasha died of typhus, she play-acted the obligatory expressions of sympathy, but the swiftness with which she then dropped them was evidence that she was more relieved than saddened. Now all she had left to do was get rid of me and

Leopold's entire, undivided future would belong to her. Her stultifying earnestness, her barren lack of humour, and her house furnished without the least bit of taste ran riot inside me like symbols of her being from another planet, and Leopold, in choosing all that, was not just betraying Wanda, he betrayed me. The man who could love such crass mundanity couldn't possibly be the same man who had taught me to love the grandeur of everything that resists mundanity.

Growing up with Leopold meant growing up on the run. Following the money, following the intrigues, moving back and forth all over Austria in search of cheaper lodgings, hiding out in Hungary, and finally fleeing to Germany, so he wouldn't have to serve the four days in jail to which the emperor had sentenced him for insulting some count. It meant wishing for the endless mobility finally to end, for the merry-go-round to come to a stop before the force with which it was spinning threw us out of the established orbit of the rest of mankind. It meant being exhausted and out of breath, gasping for air, and making only the most tentative of connections in every new town where we stayed, in order to keep it from hurting too much when we inevitably had to break them again. Growing up with Leopold meant dreaming of a home. And when those dreams finally came true, I learned to realize that dreams that come true are called disappointments. That wishes are rooted in particulars, and that when they're realized wholesale, they mean less, even quite a bit less than nothing.

When I was dreaming of a home, I certainly wasn't dreaming of Hulda Meister and her tackily furnished house out on a desolate plain where you could spot the guest you'd be entertaining in the evening as a dot on the horizon that morning. I dreamed of the home that I already had, only more solid, more certain and convincing. Of our home in Bruck, where heavy Oriental curtains took the place of doors, of that house wedged between mountains and forest, where Leopold recklessly decorated the parlour with portraits of his past lovers, deliberately arranged on the wall from least consequential to most unforgettable. Of that house, just as it was, provided we would never have to leave it. Or of our apartment in Graz, our tiny apartment in Rosenberg, where we never had anyone over, so they wouldn't suspect that Leopold's old debts were eating up any new income; of our apartment, which was too small for a family of five, and to which Leopold, who was never able to resist flattery, invited his sycophant secretary Herr Kapf, from whom he never got anything useful, Herr Kapf with the red carnation in his lapel, Herr Kapf, who could never be bothered to bathe, but who wore his hair long like a dandy, Herr Kapf, who, like Kant, took the same walk around town every day carrying his ridiculous little parasol. So many homes, so many decent homes have slipped between my fingers. Why did Lindheim, of all places, have to be the one that stuck?

There was just one thing connected to Lindheim that managed to evade my revulsion, and miraculously it was neither human, animal, nor vegetable – it was a building.

The Witch's Tower in Lindheim wasn't exactly a ruin. Quite the opposite, it seemed almost untouched, as if – like me – temporality felt some kind of restrained respect for it. In a town of trivial people and their trivial homes it was the only building that had managed to retain at least some dignity. I homed in on it as though it was a monument to everything that had vanished from my life with Wanda, and a reminder that maybe the loss was just temporary. Testimony that in this town of trivial people and their trivial homes there was nevertheless something whose measure you had to take with a much larger yardstick. Every time I left the apartment, sooner or later I would wind up standing at its base. And of course that's where I met Maximilian.

Although I had seen him approaching, when he – a complete stranger to me at that point – sat down next to me, I flinched as though he'd interrupted something.

"Have I interrupted something?" he asked.

"No, you just startled me," I said, looking him straight in the face. I recall that he struck me as handsome at the time. He was smartly dressed and his accent announced that he wasn't from around there. If only he would wave his hands a bit less when he spoke, I recall thinking.

"May I sit with you here for a bit?" he asked after he was already sitting.

"Of course," I said, "go ahead."

"Do you come here often?"

"As often as I can."

"Do you know the story behind it?" he asked, as if only the fact that I didn't know it could explain why I enjoyed spending time in this place.

Of course I knew the story of the Witch's Tower. Leopold was obsessed with it. In 1663 and 1664 the local bailiff and executioner decided that Martha Schüler, the wife of a local bigwig, had killed her own child and cooked him up into some sort of infernal brew. The story was all the more nightmarish for their having locked both her and her husband up, and while the husband managed to escape, he left her behind in the tower to be burned alive without a trial. Leopold always told this story as though it were the hagiography of that wretched, suffering woman, who had forfeited her life for nothing other than the fact that the men who surrounded her couldn't stand her greatness. What hypocrisy, I thought at the point when I hated Leopold most of all, what a devoted feminist he could be when others were involved, whereas he showed no signs of a bad conscience about dropping Wanda and letting her wander the world with no visible means of support.

"No," I replied to Maximilian, "I don't know the story."

I wanted to hear how he'd tell it. I wanted him to prove himself to me, that young man with the thick head of brown hair, with the gentle brown eyes and yesterday's beard, that phenomenon, that rift in the gaunt boredom of Hulda's Lindheim. I wanted to give him a chance.

Maximilian was a Viennese born and bred. He spent the summers in Lindheim, because his aunt – his father's sister – had married a count from there. At first he visited reluctantly, an abandoned child whose parents dropped him off here in the middle of nowhere like some object they no longer needed, because they liked to vacation in the south of Italy and they liked to vacation alone. At first he visited reluctantly, but then he learned that Sacher-Masoch had moved to Lindheim, and Maximilian worshipped Sacher-Masoch. The greatest writer after Goethe, as he was fond of saying. What a strange comparison, I recall thinking, particularly considering the fact that Leopold privately, sometimes even publicly opined that Germans were short on intellect and it would have pained him no end if he'd ever heard himself being compared to one of them, even if it was their greatest .

And yet, soon Leopold and Maximilian worshipped each other. They were just enough alike to be able to understand one another, and yet just different enough that they could exalt the things that set them apart. Leopold was reckless, which on his better days could come across as free-spiritedness, while Maximilian was painfully pedantic, which more lenient observers could interpret as a sign of reliability. At the time both still viewed themselves as philosophers, aesthetes and atheists, identities that filled them with pride. Maximilian was just then developing into a passionate reader of Rousseau, and Leopold, a veteran in that respect, took a delight in treating him to insights from his own readings of Rousseau long past. Although I still resented and was hostile towards Leopold, their unforced affinity for each other lifted my spirits. If Leopold saw something in this man who had taken to visiting our house, I thought, then perhaps I was right in deciding to give him a chance.

Hulda, too – even she worshipped Maximilian, although it would have been impossible to say if she didn't really just cherish the prospect of getting rid of my presence with the least possible effort. Hold onto that man, she liked to say, and just be grateful that there's somebody willing to love you as beautiful in spite of those mannish Slavic cheekbones of yours.

What Hulda took for love was his alacrity in adjusting his schedule so there was always time left for me, as well as the fact that he never stinted in lavishing praise on me in public. I had to admit that Maximilian always showed a keen sense for the public image of love, and yet – whether because of his natural reserve, or because he was simply, constitutionally incapable of any more genuine feeling, I never got any real sense that he loved me. I only ever got the sense that he had decided to be in love.

Maximilian, as I concluded much later, had decided that he needed to love me, because he had imagined the kind of wife for himself that other husbands lacked. A wife whose role as a painstakingly selected fashion accessory would unmistakeably attest to his rare taste, his originality and broadmindedness. A woman not just with an unpronounceable name and impossible hair, but who was the intellectual heiress of Sacher-Moser into the bargain.

But while I learned early on to doubt that his love was directed at me, as opposed to something I was supposed to represent, it would be unfair to say that doubt was all that I felt. In spite of it all, in that town of dead things, Maximilian seemed to be the only living reality. Wasn't it possible that the qualms I felt as he sat at the table, graciously chatting with my new family, were just an extension of my distrust of Leopold? Maybe those doubts weren't the kind of thing a person ought to pursue, I forced myself to believe, so instead,

I decided to pursue hope. Besides which, maybe there really wasn't anyone else who would be prepared to love me.

But to return just for a moment to that first encounter of ours, let's also recall that despite my decision to concede the narrative space and let him present the story of the Witch's Tower on his own terms, I couldn't keep the promise that I'd made to myself.

"Once, a long time ago," Maximilian began the story as though he were narrating a fairy tale.

In 1664, I almost added, but then remembered that I had already decided to lie, and that now I was going to have abide by my decision.

Still, it wasn't just that 1664 didn't come under the category of "once, a long time ago" to my way of thinking, it was also the fact that Maximilian's facile appropriation of a story that was so intimately connected to the life and death of a real, historical woman as though she were a fairy tale figure infuriated me so much that I couldn't coherently play the role that I'd decided to take on. Listening to Maximilian tell the story of the Witch's Tower, it was as though I were listening to Leopold regale an audience with stories about me as the wild child, and the flash of anger that I would have felt towards Leopold suddenly flared, grazing him, too. Maybe it would have singed any man sitting in his place at that moment, maybe at that point Maximilian wasn't yet guilty of anything at all. Maybe he was just trying to impress me. Maybe he was just yielding to something over which he had no control. I don't know which it was, but it had to come to a stop as long as I was still breathing.

"I lied," I said.

"I beg your pardon?"

"Of course I know the story of the Witch's Tower. And it didn't take place 'once, a long time ago,' it began in 1664. Surely you don't think I'm completely ignorant?"

"Please don't be angry," Maximilian said.

"How could I not be angry when you were about to take the story of a woman whose life was cut short by hatefulness and stupidity and serve it up to me as some fairy tale?"

And it was then I learned something I'd known nothing about until then. I learned that you can use kindness to wriggle your way out of an unpleasant situation.

"You're so pretty," Maximilian said, as his right hand needlessly smoothed back a strand of my hair.

I could feel the tall flame of my fury getting shorter.

Hulda had made it so nose-on-my-face clear there was nothing about me that anyone could interpret as pretty, that Maximilian's gesture took me completely by surprise.

And thus, amid the dense German fog, the Witch's Tower in Lindheim was transformed into a place of memory where my life broke into a before and an after.

"And now," Freud said to me after I first told him my story about Lindheim, "instead of focusing on the conclusions that you've formed as an adult about your process of growing up, why don't you try to remember what it was you really experienced then?"

I heaved a deep sigh.

"How do you mean?" I asked.

"This is not going to be easy," Freud replied.

3 If I try to think back on whether our relationship had anything to do with love, I can't really say that we never loved each other, although that might be the easiest response. We were in love, but our love was a matter of solitude. Each of us experienced it separately, only for it to vanish on the day when we took up with each other again.

It even started out unfortunately. Maximilian said that he loved me, his hands flitting around a bit more than I would have preferred.

I said I agreed with that, and then he went off to do his military service and I promised to wait for him.

That was the year when Leopold completely withdrew. The year when, without even trying to conceal the fact, he began to lock himself away in his study with Hulda's maid Bertha, a forty-year-old Bavarian woman with broad shoulders and palms like a farmhand's. The year when we only ever heard his voice in the sequences of screams that coincided with the lashes of the whip behind closed doors. The only living being he showed any kindness to was Mimi, a grey tabby cat that let nobody near her except him. Whenever he would sit in his armchair of an evening, smoking in silence, she would sit in his lap and purr. Sometimes I watched them through the crack in the door as I tried to guess what had triggered Leopold's regression. If he hadn't gone mad at the death of his heir, his beloved son Sasha, why now? Was it possible his madness was the result of my upcoming departure, or was I assuming too large a role for myself?

Even if it wasn't possible to determine the cause of Leopold's insanity, it was all too easy to measure its impact. It had become the nucleus of Hulda's household and it was clear from the look in his eyes as they refused to engage you, or from his sparse sentences that now only communicated what there was no denying, that his decision to go public with his need for pain was no sign of trust. It was a betrayal, plain and simple. Old and exhausted, Leopold could no longer muster the energy to impersonate a husband, a father, a friend engaging you in conversation, a human being. He became one with his illness. To this day I'm convinced it was catastrophic for Hulda, but if I'm to be perfectly honest, I don't recall mourning for him. I suppose I've deliberately forgotten. But you need to know that at that time I was probably the only person (with the possible exception of Bertha – but then, who really knows what servants feel, anyway?)

who had the means to protect herself from being overwhelmed by the atmosphere of despondency that Leopold was dictating.

It wasn't just that in the course of the years since Leopold and Wanda had split up, since my childhood had ceased to resemble my childhood and had become the childhood of somebody else who did her French homework and defied her stepmother while living in a tiny house in some remote German province – it wasn't just that I had already done my share of mourning. Or that that I had already been missing Leopold, my tutor and teacher, for so long that I couldn't miss him any more. Or that I had an advantage on Hulda, because my recovery began sooner or because living with him had never been a matter of choice for me, something that *ipso facto* washed away any guilt. It was that I'd let myself get distracted by love and the anticipation of a life that had yet to take shape. In love, that most spectacular of all spectacular escapes, I would finally become my own future – this was something I had to believe. I was eighteen years old. Nearly ten years had passed since the days when Leopold would remind me each week that one day, when I grew up, I would become a historical personage. At that time I was still just a country girl who put all her hopes in marrying someone she barely knew.

If I'd had eyes to see, I would have noticed that that was also the year of Hulda's defeat. I would have seen her sitting alone at the dining-room table, her eyes fixed on the landscape paintings on the wall, I would have seen her rearranging the books in the library, wiping the dust off them, even though Bertha had just done a thorough job of that moments before. If I'd had eyes to see, and an attention span that I was willing to share, I would have realized that that was the year when Hulda was forced to admit that she'd made a mistake. The year when that woman, who had always been so capable of discerning right from wrong, was forced to realize that she could no longer view herself as a person who made nothing but rational decisions in life, and whom the world would naturally have to reward with happiness. The year when she realized that, no, she hadn't become the wife of a famous writer, whom history would accord a place in its voluminous tomes, but rather that she'd married a man who was so focused on his infirmity that she would have to tend to him, unrecognized, to her dying day. The year when Hulda realized she wasn't that different from Wanda, although her petit-bourgeois vanity kept her from ever saying so out loud.

But Hulda was the last thing that seemed worth thinking about at the time. I was superficial and detached, and more than anything else I thought of Leopold as a burden that I was unable to drive from my thoughts in order to free up as much space as love would require. If I was going to credit the world with the beauty that would come my way with the promise of its realization, I had to look past quite a bit, and in particular past the people I lived with.

That's why I was going to have to isolate myself, too. Lindheim lacked the dimensions of a city, it was too small for a person to submerge in. Once you stepped out your door and went down the street, you weren't vanishing in the crowd, you were simply expanding the inner circle of your family out into the wider locality, encountering people who always knew in advance how you were, or rather, how you ought to be, given what was being said about you behind your back, and yet would politely ask you how you were doing. That's why I went for long, remote walks, until the fields and boundary stones separating the world of human things from the world of all other things gave way to forests.

Alone, I wanted to be alone, I wanted to get away from the gossip that so uselessly crowded my thoughts, which were too precious not to deserve my full and undivided attention. I would leave Hulda's house in the morning and not come home until the sounds of the night creatures had begun to inform me that day had come to a definite close. The forest, that dense patch of uncultivated world, didn't figure for me as a threat as I made my way home through the twilight. I saw it as the backdrop to my emotional life, that impenetrable undergrowth of desires that I had never before wished for and that I had to discover anew. But maybe, I would say to myself, for the first time secretly proud of the complicated story of my childhood, I really am the wild child that Leopold had invented. If somebody else had been able to assess my value and view me as a rarity from a museum collection, why shouldn't I be able to feel that value as an integral part of myself?

The future before me unfolded as definite plans: I would go back to Austria, that land of my memory where boredom was banned; to Vienna, which I didn't yet know, but had clearly seen in the well-read, exquisitely dressed people who listened attentively to each other and, when they said something, spoke deliberately and respectfully; I saw the house it would be my duty to furnish, I saw my wedding, the love that would become a matter of public record, and the guests that would validate it, high-spirited and envious at one and the same time; my children, my daughter, her happiness, brains and beauty, and Maximilian, eternally murmuring how beautiful I was and how much he loved me, his kisses, his hands on my hips, his tenderness, devotion and undivided attention. Did I see Leopold getting better? Waking up from difficult dreams, shaking his head and smiling, hugging me and saying how happy he was for me? Or did I try to think him away?

Every so often a letter arrived, testifying that Maximilian hadn't forgotten. He had plans, too, and by all accounts they weren't that much different from mine. He would come for me and take me with him to Vienna, he would become my husband, give me a house to furnish, children to raise, and love to use. We were writing on the same subjects, but the difference in styles couldn't have escaped

reader. I indulged my emotions in a most inhospitable
e pragmatically set forth all sorts of plans, and in the
newness of our love neither one of us noticed that we were staring
at each other across an abyss.

When, about a week before Maximilian's return, I was coming
back from a walk, I saw Leopold sitting outside the house and
crying. Mimi lay lifeless in his arms. His fingers were covered with
ink, and it was as though they were dripping with thick, dark blood.

Leopold was a neurotic, a hypochondriac who didn't cope well
with pressures and concerns, who was wont to pace nervously back
and forth through a room, crack his knuckles and bite his nails – but
cry? Crying was something he almost never did.

"I don't know what happened," he said, sobbing. "I wanted to
write – it's been so long since I've written. Then she jumped up on
the desk and knocked over the ink. I swatted her away, but I swatted
too hard, I shouldn't have pushed her away so forcefully, I don't
know what happened."

He raised his head and looked at me. Had it been a full year, half
a year, since he last looked me in the eyes?

"Everything I touch dies, Nada, everything."

Had it been a decade since he last called me by my name?

It was as if all of his sorrow and all of his horror suddenly toppled
onto me, burying me in their inevitability. It was impossible to see
him this fragile and helpless, and it was impossible to fend off the
childish fear I would feel whenever he got overly agitated.

How hard, I wondered, do you have to swat a cat away in order
to kill it? Can you do it by accident? And if, as I sometimes believed,
I was also one of his stray cats, was he going to squash me by mistake
some day when he might try to hug me again? If I had been walking
past him through Lindheim all summer long, if I had shared the
house with him in his absence and silence, now here he was, all of

him, before me, impassable, as if his presence were warning me that if some day I did want to move into the future, I would have to do it by bypassing him.

"Come here," I said and held out my hand, so he could use it to brace himself and get up. There was no other option available, I had to be the one assuming the role of normalcy, I had to staunch my sorrows and fears and hope that it would pass over to him.

"Come, let's bury her," I said, as if assuaging a child.

Leopold set the dead cat down on the floor beside him and got up. We got a shovel and headed out through the fields towards my forest, above which the darkness was already gathering, the forest that had represented my love for so long, but was now being forced to make the tiniest bit of room for death. We buried Mimi in silence. Leopold the atheist made a little cross for her grave.

"So that the other animals know," he said.

I imagined a fox padding towards the sunrise and pausing there for a moment.

Unexpectedly Leopold embraced me. I felt a shudder as my body tautened for a moment in self-defence, even though nothing out of the ordinary was happening. Just a sad old man unloading some of his sadness onto me. In silence we walked back home.

Of all the things I imagined through the months of anticipation, I could never have imagined that Maximilian would come back home changed, and that I would welcome him home, changed myself. He arrived while I was still engulfed in grief and concern, since Leopold hadn't emerged from his study for a good week and Hulda had been wailing the whole time, and even Maximilian, whom up to that point I'd only known for his uncomplicated predisposition, came home sullen and grim. He was thin, thinner than the image of him that I nurtured in memory, and this froze the features of his face into a solemn mask.

His parents, as I learned, had died. There had been a calamity at sea. Maximilian provided no further details, because he didn't know any, himself. I'll never meet them now, I recall thinking, I'll never find out who the people were who formed him as the man I had come to know.

We were grateful for each other's company, but our happiness was buttressed by sorrow rather than joy, and apparently sorrow of necessity always separates people, so that's why we walked through the fields of late August hand in hand, but each submerged in his own silence. I wanted to show him the edge of the forest that I had made my home while I waited for him. If he could see the external circumstances that had provided a hospitable housing for my love, perhaps he would also see what love itself looked like.

The cross on the tiny grave was gone. Was that a good sign? A bad one? Any sign at all?

We sat down on the low-lying branch of a tree that appeared to be trapped between growing up into a real tree or holding fast as a bush.

"Are you sad?" I asked.

It was a stupid question, I realize, but the import of our meeting had robbed me of any last bit of prudence.

"I don't know," he said, sounding sad. "I just don't understand why anything is born if it ultimately has to die."

It was as though war and death had cut down his last bit of youthful idealism, or as though the fact that there were no more adults left to make him a child had provoked a sudden disillusionment, the way a late frost freezes buds that have begun to open too early.

I didn't have any answer for him, none that could comfort him, much less explain, all I could do was sit beside him, squeezing his hand. I knew the confusion that came with death, I knew what it meant to lose the certainty with which you had peopled your life in its absence, as if you could reasonably see yourself as its master, I knew something of the helplessness that in its vicinity seems like the world's only truth, but I knew nothing about whatever levers I might have used to bridge it. Involuntarily I remembered the day Sasha died.

Sasha was a perfect child. Leopold's favourite child – precisely because, as Wanda would have said, he was the least like him. Golden-haired, blue-eyed, and weak, he was a prince from a fairy tale. Ever since I'd been conscious of myself, he had been the object of my jealousy. Leopold and Wanda obsessively vied for his attention, each determined in his own way to play the role of the favourite parent. He was incapable of doing anything wrong. Whenever he flung his food around because it didn't meet his notions of the perfect meal for a particular occasion, Wanda would fix him something special. He was the only person who could interrupt Leopold in mid-story and chide him for being boring without any consequences. He was their first-born, a living, breathing reminder that between them there had once existed something that they were prepared to call love, he was a totem that they couldn't help idolising. If he hadn't died young, could he have conceivably grown up into a good person? Compared to him, Mitja and I, Leopold's dark little double and the wild child, were condemned to second-class status. Mitja decided very early on that he couldn't compete with his brother for their father's attention, so he focused on Wanda, becoming her consolation and confidant. In disputes he was sometimes the only one to assure her that she wasn't the one who had behaved badly, and over the years he managed to win her unshakeable love. It almost went without saying that with the divorce he belonged to her, while I, whom Leopold had told often enough was born for greatness, stubbornly kept competing. My jealousy of Sasha became practically the most characteristic feature of my childhood. Why should I have accepted second place? Because I wasn't his? Because I was a girl?

Suddenly he fell ill. In my childish cruelty I followed his illness with envy, too. Of course, I thought, of course Sasha had come up with a way of once again refocusing all the attention on himself. The whole house became his shrine. Leopold summoned the best physician from Frankfurt, and even Hulda sat at his bedside night and day, reading to him. Weeks had to go by and Sasha had to become practically transparent before I realized that his illness wasn't something a person could deliberately fake. On the eve of his death, when he lapsed into a fevered delirium, I prayed for the first and last time in my life. Leopold was a thoroughgoing atheist. Consequently, none of his children had been educated in the art of prayer, and I, eyes tearful and nerves frayed, had no idea what I needed to do to make it effective. I knelt down beside my bed, the way I imagined it was done, clasped my hands together and tried to come up with something convincing. Please, please, please let Sasha live, I kept repeating, I was wrong, I was wicked, but now I see how wrong I was. Please let everything turn out all right, it can still turn out all right, can't it? But it didn't, it all went bad. Towards morning Sasha died and all the energy that had driven my jealousy up to that point was converted to guilt. Was I at fault for his dying? Would he have lived if I had loved him more? Was Leopold going to hate me for not having died in his place? Someone had died, my brother had died, while I in my childish egocentricity could still only see myself.

And even now, I suddenly thought, next to the man I should love, who's consumed by his grief, I can only think of myself.

"Tell me about them," I said.

Maximilian shook his head.

"I can't. I can't think of them without thinking that I'll never see them again."

He was silent for a while, and then he repeated the old refrain: "was it my fault? If I'd been with them, would they have lived?"

My garden of love, the place I had brought him to in order for nature to show him what I was feeling, the place I had cut off from the world in order to fill it with my own emotions, had suddenly become saturated with death.

I gave him a kiss. If my family was descending into decadence and if his was succumbing to death, the two of us would just have to learn how to be a family for each other.

He toppled me off the branch, wedging me between himself and the chill ground, kissing me, like a starving man gulping down bits of bread. As though I weren't even really there, while looking past his head I noticed that night, sharp and bright, had fallen over the forest.

I wished I could feel differently, but all I could feel was the dry twigs cutting into my skin and the long, deep distance in the painful intimacy between us.

4 "Welcome home, Mrs. Moser," Maximilian said as he escorted me across the threshold of the house on the Spiegelgasse, the house of his father, his house, our house. The biggest house I had ever lived in, which, unlike the apartments and refurbished mills that Leopold had rented, testified to the fact that the Mosers weren't just aristocrats by virtue of title, but by their way of life. Three floors, a ballroom with piano, a dining room with a freshly polished oak table and serious Flemish-style still lifes hanging on the walls.

"It's exquisite," I said, as I'd been taught.

It was the kind of house that deserves high praise. A serious house, built with serious people in mind. What on earth could it have had to do with me?

Because I had spent nineteen years living with a name that didn't belong to me by blood, I never believed that any organic connection existed between things and their names, so whenever somebody called me Mrs. Moser, even if it was just Maximilian, my husband, the man I was now bound to in a meaningful relationship, it was as though they were talking about somebody else. I knew Nadezhda Sacher-Masoch. To a large extent she consisted of uncertainty and doubts, but those were familiar, comfortable, oversized doubts. But who was Nadezhda Moser? In my new name, in Maximilian's house, in Vienna, in everything I felt like an intruder. Welcome home, Mrs. Moser. It sounded like a joke at my expense.

If you can't feel gratitude, I said to myself in Hulda's voice, you can at least try to pretend.

"It's wonderful," I said and kissed him at the foot of the stairs, my hands clasped around his neck.

"Are you happy?" he asked.

I nodded. So why wasn't I happy?

I had everything that the adults who raised me ascribed any value to: a husband with money the way Hulda imagined him, a husband who insisted on loving me unconditionally, as Wanda had wished for, I was in the heart of Austria, the heart of the world, the heart of life, as Leopold had wanted to be. Was anything wrong?

In Lindheim Leopold liked to play the part of the exile dreaming of an Austria he would never be able to see again. In fact, the reality was much more banal. He could have gone back whenever he wanted. All he would have needed to do was serve four full days in jail. Four days. To this day I can't say if it was fear or pride or just cold feet at the thought of the grotesquely oversized jail rats, fear of the plague he would have caught from them, fear of the other prisoners, aggressive he-men who would have beaten him to death before the first day was over. Or was it that he couldn't picture himself as someone with a prison record? Was it his social amour-propre that got in the way? Or the memory of his father, the police inspector? Or was it simply that he thought the verdict was unjust?

I recall how he dispatched Wanda to an audience with the emperor to plead clemency for him. And how in her absence she was suddenly replaced in our apartment in Leipzig by Hulda, who at the time was still Leopold's petit-bourgeois secretary from the German provinces. I remember, as if it were yesterday, how I woke up one morning to find her installed right in the middle of my juvenile life, seated at the family table as though she belonged there with some sort of natural urgency. Would she vanish when Wanda got back? Let her, I hoped. But Hulda remained. She stayed longer than I did. But at the time I couldn't have foreseen any of that.

Leopold had to instruct Hulda to keep a low profile until he had time to resolve his own situation. Either that, or she was just naturally discreet, but whatever the reason, when Wanda got back, Hulda was nowhere to be seen. It was a late August evening, both warm and cool at the same time. Leopold was sitting in his leather-upholstered armchair. Wanda had set her tiny suitcase on the floor by her feet and was sitting across from him. Neither one of them knew that I was hiding in the wardrobe.

"The emperor," Wanda began, "is unable to do anything. He wants you to know that he will always see you as one of his most devoted subjects, and he will always be grateful for what you've done for the empire, but there's nothing he can do about your sentence. I wouldn't care, he said, for posterity to remember me as an emperor who was ready to ride roughshod over the laws when it suited him."

Was she lying? Had she even had an audience with the emperor? It was all too easy for me to imagine her lying dressed on her bed in the Hotel Imperial, reading, enjoying the space she was occupying, enjoying the quiet and the fact that nobody was expecting her to wait on them, thinking about how nice it would be to have enough money to never have to go home again. Lounging on the bed and reading, reading and lounging, and never doing what Leopold had asked her to do, as if determined to punish him.

"We need to talk," Leopold said.

In the history of mankind had those words ever been followed by anything good?

"Oh?" Wanda said quizzically.

"I know you're sleeping with Armand."

At the time Armand, who later turned out to be a Jewish con-man named Jacob Rosenthal, was passing himself off as a man of means with some interest in playing the role of publisher for Leopold's pet publishing project, a journal. We met him when we first moved to Leipzig, almost at the same time as we met Hulda, and like Hulda, he immediately became a regular fixture in our household. He was elegant, well dressed and a smooth talker.

The expression on Wanda's face vacillated between surprise and disbelief.

"Leopold, I beg you," she said.

"I know you, Wanda, and I know you wouldn't have slept with him if you didn't love him, and I can't live with a woman who loves someone else."

"Why, Leopold, you son of a bitch," Wanda said. She was angry. Had I ever seen her angry before? Come to think of it now, at that moment she must have loved somebody else in order to direct all that anger at Leopold, whom she had always been loath to offend, as long as she loved him.

"So it's true," Leopold said with exaggerated regret in his voice.

"Do you know what I think?' Wanda said.

"No, what?" Leopold replied. He didn't know.

"I think you're fucking your secretary and now you're looking for a handy excuse to get rid of me."

"Wanda, don't be vulgar," Leopold said solemnly. "And please speak of Miss Meister with a bit more respect."

"Oh, come on, stop pretending," Wanda said, "it doesn't become you."

"I don't know what you're talking about. And please don't judge others by your own standards."

Plastered to the back of the wardrobe, I was biting my hand. What was going on? Why was Leopold behaving as if the whole business with Hulda was made up? Why was he acting as though Wanda was crazy? Why was he foisting all of the guilt onto her? Was that even allowed?

"Do you know what disgusts me most about you, Leopold?" Wanda suddenly asked. "It's the fact that you insist on playing the victim even when you're at fault for everything."

"Please, calm down."

"What for? So that you don't have to deal with this? Because you think it's perfectly natural for you to do what you want, while the rest of us have to accommodate you, as if we had no will of our own?"

Wanda, who even in her manner of speech had always done her best to impersonate a lady who deserved to be married to an aristocrat, suddenly dropped all pretence. She was crying, but there was no discernible sorrow in what she said. Only a long-suppressed fury.

"Wanda, you're being hysterical. I can't speak to you when you're like this."

"You don't even want to talk. You want to tell me what I have to do so your life will be the way you've imagined it," she said, picking her suitcase up off the floor and heading back out the door she'd come in through.

Leopold remained sitting at the table, lost in thought.

My knees had been weakened from their forced immobility and my cheeks were running with tears. I had to exert all of my effort to keep from snorting out loud.

Just under a week later everything was decided. Nothing would come out in the paper. Wanda and Mitja would move to Paris with Armand. Leopold, Sasha and I would move to Lindheim with Hulda. I was still crying as we left Leipzig riding in Hulda's carriage.

"Don't cry," Hulda said. "You'll upset your father."

But Leopold hardly seemed upset. Everything had played out pretty much as he had envisioned. Except that he still couldn't return to Austria, and the thing that most grieved him about that was that Austria itself hadn't tried harder to get him back. After all, wasn't he one of her favourite sons? His love of Austria, combined with what he perceived as its rejection of him, engendered resentment, even if it wasn't so strong that he ever forgot that his homeland was grander than others in every respect, and certainly a lot grander than dreary Germany, which now assumed for him the likeness of Lindheim. Even though he had moved there willingly and even though his pursuit of Hulda, who with nearly incomprehensible self-abnegation sought only to look after him, brought him advantages without end, even Leopold couldn't be generous about Lindheim. When he met Maximilian, he also advised me to stick with him.

"That man is going to take you to Vienna!" he said, as if that were some sort of particularly precious reward.

As Leopold conceived of it, Vienna was a metaphor for Austria, while Austria was a metaphor for everything that was conceivably beautiful about humankind. It would have been impossible to unify it, and that was what Leopold adored. It was the embodiment of diversity, dynamism embodied, the very opposite of ennui. Sometimes I wondered how his adulation of Austrian diversity could coexist with his pan-Slavic fairy tale, but I soon came to understand that Leopold was not one to let contradictions limit him.

"That man is going to take you to Vienna! I've always been happy in Vienna," he said, even though that was hardly the truth. A financial debacle in Vienna had nearly led to the loss of his entire fortune. His first child – the one he had forced himself to forget about so that Sasha could serve as his first-born – had died in Vienna. Clearly the beauty of Vienna was so great that even the most inconceivable pain was no match for it. It was easy to indulge this image of perfection that the future promised to bring.

And now that man, my husband, had actually brought me to Vienna. Why couldn't I feel this as the reward that had been promised to me?

At the doorway into the salon Maximilian introduced me to the servants. They were lined up in order of height, arranged like silverware, like some prized possession that fills its owner with pride, like painstakingly collected objects that attest to the expertise and good taste of the collector, which turn a house into a home, and a home into a monument to the personality of the individual who resides there. From the tallest on the left to the shortest on the right I was looking at the coachman, the valet, the cook, two maids, and a tiny girl who was assigned to me.

"That's Ruslana," Maximilian said. "She's Ruthenian, also from Lemberg."

"From Kolomiya, sir," the Ruthenian said as she made a slight curtsey. Her voice sounded as though it belonged to a taller, stouter, wealthier woman. Leopold would have liked this one for sure, I thought. Although overall she seemed fragile, her hands and arms appeared to be large and muscular.

"Ruslana," Maximilian said, glancing her way with a slight tilt of his head. His body expressed a mixture of surprise and anger.

"I would like you to remember something. You must never, and when I say never, I mean never embarrass your master in public. You're here to help, not hinder."

"I understand, sir, forgive me," she said. Her apology sounded complete, although her face showed no sign of regret.

"Very good. If my wife is prepared to give you a second chance, you shall have a second chance. But mind you, there will be no third chance. Nada?"

He stood facing them, my husband did, facing his assembled army in their impeccable uniforms, their faces straining to reveal as little as possible, their hands manicured, their shoes shined, he stood facing his workers, whose appearance he doted upon more than most fallen aristocrats could afford to do, facing these people who were forced to comply with his every demand, his every wish, no matter how nonsensical it might be, he stood before them completely at ease, as if there were something natural about that order of things, waiting for me to decide.

Everything I know about life I've learned from servants, was something Leopold liked to say. Reading, writing, understanding people and their nature, telling stories. He would never have become a writer without the education he got from his family's Ukrainian servants. His father had lived in his office, while his mother lived in her canopied bed, and Leopold never forgot that, if not for their servants, he would have been alone and deprived of direction. He adored his mother, although I several times heard him say that he'd had more meaningful conversation with his nanny than with her. He had liked the servants. He enjoyed talking to them and drinking with them, and he never drew a sharp line between them and himself. Even before he squandered most of his money, he was convinced that class distinctions would have to be abolished. "People are people," he used to say. No wonder he married a seamstress.

Wanda never forgot she was one of them. She treated our chambermaids and my governesses (who rarely stayed on for more than a month, particularly the young and pretty ones) as though she was one of them. She could be jealous and envious of them, since they were her closest competitors, and she always kept an eye out for whether Leopold might be on the verge of leaving her for one of them, and she was right to do so. Leopold was fond of the manservants, but there was none he was fonder of than any of the women.

Hulda had Bertha, towards whom she could be domineering, but that always came across as though she were addressing a younger sister who wasn't always capable of discerning right from wrong.

But then came Maximilian. He was the first person in my life who knew how to rule over people. I could tell from the look on his face that he expected as much from me. Was this some kind of test?

I felt uncomfortable. I had never before been strict with anyone, nor did I want to be, but I also didn't want to disappoint Maximilian. I think I didn't want him to be angry with me. I wanted to meet his expectations.

I stood there, as though my feet had shot dense, powerful roots into the floor. I didn't know what to do.

"Well?" Maximilian asked.

I smiled benevolently. "It's all right," I said. Was I supposed to say anything more?

"You're in luck, my wife is soft-hearted," he said to Ruslana.

Ruslana nodded.

"Company dismissed," Maximilian said, and the servants dispersed to continue about their tasks.

"If you're too easy on them, they're going to eat you alive," Maximilian said, almost in jest. Had he been this cruel from the start, and I just hadn't noticed?

I nodded.

"Forgive me," I said.

"It's all right," he said, kissing me on the forehead. "Now let me show you your new rooms."

I was assigned a corner room in the left wing of the third floor. It was well lit through big windows looking onto the street, a massive wooden wardrobe and a huge raised bed. This was the promise of solitude that I had never before experienced, consigned as I'd always been to rooms that had always been at least a little too small.

"It's wonderful," I repeated, except that this time it cost me no effort to strike the right tone. This was my room and I fell in love with it at once. Maybe everything will turn out all right after all, I thought. Just think of all the beautiful, unexpected things still in store. I just have to get used to a few things. If as a child I'd grown used to constant changes of address, over the past few years I'd grown somehow settled in Lindheim, and even though I had an aversion to it, it was strange to leave there. And it was strange to leave Leopold. Every step through the streets of Vienna and every step up the stairs in Maximilian's house was a step into the unknown, where every next step could very well be into the void. I knew nothing about the ground I was treading, consequently I could anticipate nothing. Perhaps this time it was not so much a matter of my being unhappy. I was scared. Everything was so new, so big, so beyond comprehending. I was in alien territory. And I needed time before I could begin thinking of that as something exciting.

"Very good," Maximilian said, kissing me on the forehead. "Get some rest, you'll need to be fresh this evening, or Helene will feel put out."

Helene and Wolfgang, Maximilian's sister and her husband, were responsible for the social component of my move to Vienna. For the past month Helene had been planning a party that would enable me to meet everyone she thought I might need to know. Is that what had put me out of sorts? Was it worrying me?

"Don't worry," I said.

"I'm not worried about a thing," Maximilian assured me, squeezing my hand.

How nice for you, I thought, smiling and closing the door behind him.

5 "I can't possibly thank you enough," I told Helene when we kissed at the door. "You don't need to throw a party just on account of me."

"Are you joking? Of course I do. What else am I supposed to do – leave the planning to Maximilian? Especially now, with him so tense about everything? He's acting as though he's taken the place of our father."

"Please, Helene," Maximilian said. He really did sound tense.

Until I met Helene and Wolfgang, I'd never thought of Maximilian as particularly divided, but watching the two of them was like watching Maximilian split into two different people. She was casual and chatty, light-hearted and kind, giving the impression of someone who was completely in and of the world, as though in her presence the very concept of solitude evaporated. He, by contrast, was restrained and conscientious, and although I never saw him peevish or gruff, the expression on his face bespoke the tension that he continually had to absorb to keep the world around him from falling apart. Her entire manner was about resistance to strictures, while his was all about maintaining order, and if she brought a touch of buoyancy to his life, he kept hers on the safe side of insanity. They gave the impression of harmony, Helene and Wolfgang. How lucky that they found each other, the gossips might say. When I first got to know them, my first thought about Wolfgang was whether it was hard for him to maintain that internal equilibrium. Had he perhaps, as each year added new responsibilities to his burdens, come to let certain parts of himself express themselves less and less often? Was that why he had become what Helene interpreted as peevish? Did he feel all that time as though he'd had to forsake something? I glanced at him a few times. His face expressed nothing.

"Come in, come in," Helene said, "you can't just stand in the doorway all evening."

She had auburn hair and she was wearing a long, pink dress with an Oriental pattern. Was it possible she didn't wear a corset?

"Walk with me," she said, "I'll introduce you."

"Are you having a good time?" she asked as we made our way from the entrance hall to the salon. When I got to know her a little better, I realized that the whole house in which she and Wolfgang lived carried her imprint. It was as delightful as she was, and like her it boasted exceptional taste. It didn't have the slightest trace of the seriousness that characterized my new domicile on the Spiegelgasse. Her furniture was as modern as her dress, designed for comfort and fun. Both she and her house were the very embodiments of hospitality.

I nodded. Even though the floor beneath my feet wavered in uncertainty, in some sense I really was having a good time.

"Emilie!" she suddenly exclaimed, waving to a redhead with curls who had just then entered the salon, wearing a light blue dress embroidered with gold that was in every detail apart from its colour identical to the one Helene was wearing herself, and likewise not wearing a corset. She joined us and she and Helene exchanged affectionate kisses.

"Emilie, this is my new sister. Isn't she divine? We've got to ask Klimt to do her portrait. If she'll agree, of course."

"I'm afraid," the redhead began, "I'll never have enough influence to forbid him anything… Emilie Flöge," she said, extending her hand to me.

"Emilie is a wonderful artist," Helene interjected.

"Seamstress would be the more appropriate term," Emilie added.

"Oh, don't be so modest, it doesn't suit you at all. A lot of us can't wait for Emilie to open the first salon suitable for humans in this town that fashion forgot."

"I just need to save a bit more change," Emilie said, smiling.

"This is her masterpiece," Helene said, doing a light turn in her pink dress. "We've got to get one of these for you, too."

Emilie sized me up with an expert eye. "I see you're still using a corset," she said. She was displeased. "It's so hard to convince Austrian women to give them up." There was something funny about the matter-of-fact way she lumped me in with "Austrians." Something I was not used to at all. Something that both appealed to and offended me at the same time.

"Friedrich's cousin recently told me," she continued, "that her corset keeps her together. As though she'd come flying apart if she didn't have to endure it some day."

I didn't know the Friedrich in question, much less his cousin, but I think I knew what she was trying to say. Perhaps she also lived in a world that for years had been threatening to go flying apart, and she needed something to hold it together from the outside. Like Maximilian, I thought. There was also something funny about the sudden realization that it took appreciating the fashion choices of some Viennese woman I'd only just now heard about for me to recognize the similarity with the bond I felt to my own husband. Where was he anyway, that husband of mine? I suddenly wanted him to be standing beside me.

I left Helene in Emilie's care and went to find Maximilian sur-rounded by men. Like Wolfgang, all of them were medical doctors, but all were advancing in years and deep down in the furrows on their faces, all of which were indistinguishable from each other, there were thick layers of arrogance and complacency. Just as Wolfgang and Helene had split into two, so had their social circles, with Wolfgang's half clearly consisting of people he hoped to impress. As, one after the other, they kissed my hand and told me their surnames, which, one after the other, I immediately proceeded to forget, I began to regret my decision to join Maximilian. Like Wolfgang, he looked like a schoolboy amid this assembly of wise men.

"We've heard so much about you, Mrs. Moser," the first wise man said. "I'm so pleased to finally have the honour of meeting you."

Whatever these people had heard about me, it couldn't have been anything good.

"Do you know," another one said, "some years ago I also had a wild child in my care. It all ended so sadly, you know." He spoke so poorly, he could barely get a word out and what he did say was so guttural, it was as if he were speaking Dutch.

At this point all of them gave a forced laugh.

"At any rate, to cut a long story short, at age thirteen he was found hanging, poor boy. But you, you appear to be amazingly civilized with no signs of an inclination to suicide," he continued, as if a propensity to commit suicide were the equivalent of a common cold.

"Strictly speaking," I said, noticing through the corner of my eye that Maximilian's face was distorted into a threatening grimace that was trying to warn me to be careful in choosing my words, "I'm not a wild child. I was several days old when they found me."

Even before my words had faded away, Maximilian picked up on them by other means.

"Gentlemen," he said, "my wife has a gift for humility."

I could feel goose bumps rising on the back of my neck.

"It is often a source of amazement to me how the fact that she lived the most vulnerable years of her childhood without the company of people is in no way reflected by her behaviour. I am convinced that if any one of the rest of us were left abandoned as infants in the middle of a forest until we were found, not a single one would have developed intelligence beyond the level of an imbecile. I would even dare to say that her normalcy is proof of superior intelligence."

I realize that Maximilian intended everything he said as a compliment, but the more he praised that invented person, that noble savage girl, the more he insulted me, the flesh and blood person standing beside him. Was that how cows felt when they were auctioned at fairs?

"Well," the first wise man continued, "I don't doubt for a second that your wife is exceptional, but let me suggest that her upbringing had something to do with that, wouldn't you say?"

For a moment I was grateful to him for redirecting the conversation from me and at least momentarily returning it to the realm of normality, but that moment was over all too soon.

"Although it's interesting, considering who did educate you, don't you think?" said a third wise man who had been silent until then.

"What do you mean by that?" I asked stupidly, even though I knew very well what he meant by that. How can you be normal, when you come from a household of lunatics? That has to mean that you're not normal after all, doesn't it? Wouldn't you agree?

"I mean, I don't mean to offend you, and I never knew your father intimately and wouldn't want to be unfair to him, but I have read some Krafft-Ebing, you know, that chapter in his *Psychopathia Sexualis*. Have you read it?"

"No, I haven't," I said, even though I had. We all had to read selected passages from *Psychopathia Sexualis*, even the children, all of us had to listen to Leopold rage against some "clinical worm" who had branded his work as an "outright expression of perversity". What perversity? And what's the problem with these people? Don't they know how complicated human nature is? Do they not know that pleasure and pain are always inextricably linked in us? Of course they don't know, because they're a bunch of Catholic mediocrities. How could they know, when they've never even dared to glance into the abyss of the human soul? So they need to punish the only person who's dared? And brand him an idiot? Of course I'd read *Psychopathia Sexualis*, I'd read it as soon as I'd learned how to read, but I preferred not to argue. Did Maximilian not notice how uncomfortable I was? Was he unable to do anything to put an end to this torture?

"Well, in brief, Krafft-Ebing thought that your father not only described these perversions, but that he also suffered from some of their symptoms, for instance, that he enjoyed letting ladies beat him, especially when he was bound, you see – and I simply thought it was interesting that someone who obviously had so many problems of his own could be such an exceptional pedagogue."

"Oh, come now, Weibl," said the first wise man, who was clearly the most lenient member of this ancient Greek chorus weighing in on my character and upbringing. "So what does the fact that somebody lets himself get tied to a pole and kicked by gentle ladies' feet say about the person at all? Why, you patronize whores yourself, and yet you treat men for syphilis, and nobody asks how you reconcile your internal contradictions."

The third wise man went red in the face.

"There you go," said Wolfgang, who had wisely stayed silent until then. "You could at least mind your language in the presence of a lady."

Minding one's language meant not saying "whore," but it didn't mean not putting the lady in a position where she felt like a circus animal. It was an opportune moment to leave. I tried to give Maximilian a pleading glance, but he was looking away and refused to be bothered.

Then the second wise man spoke up again.

"I don't mean to embarrass you," he said, although it was obvious that he couldn't care less whether he embarrassed me or not, "but – you've lived with Sacher-Masoch, you know these things first hand. Would you say there's any truth to what Krafft-Ebing writes about him?"

I was quietly still hoping that Maximilian would jump in, that he'd intervene to stop the course of the conversation, which had managed to shift from awkward to agonizing. Was it permissible to ask questions like these? What had happened to the time-honoured practise of gossiping about people behind their backs? After some incredibly long moments of silence I realized that I was in this fray without any allies and that I would have to find my way out of it on my own. I imagined Leopold paying my governess and the cook to go play robbers with him, or hunters and bear, which in either case involved their waiting behind some trees, wooden bats in hand, for him to pass by as he strolled through the orchard, so that they could jump out, knock him to the ground and give him a good drubbing until he lost consciousness. I imagined him helping Wanda into her muskrat fur coat to teach her the fine art of looking down her nose at him. I imagined him having a perfectly good tooth yanked out in spite of the dentist's entreaties for him to reconsider. Of course all of the things that Krafft-Ebing had written about were true, although he did a poor job of explaining them, but every fibre of my being resisted conceding to these clinical worms that they were right. Suddenly, the cause of defending Leopold's honour and, with it, my own, acquired the utmost importance, even if it meant I was going to have to lie about it.

"Let me remind you again," I finally said, "that it's hard for me to pass judgement on any of this, because I haven't read *Psychopathia Sexualis*, but judging by what you've described, I would have to say there's been a good deal of exaggerating going on."

I could feel the veins in my forehead grow taut with the strain and picked up the sour smell of sweat seeping through my perfume, but I had the sense that I'd carried it off.

The wise men nodded. Apparently my response had satisfied them, too.

"I'm tired," I said to Maximilian, "do you think we could go soon?"

He looked at me with a split second's delay, as though just then startled awake.

"Of course," he said once he'd fully come to. "Gentlemen, the lady's wish is my command."

The wise men nodded once again. Wolfgang offered to see us to the door.

"Did you have a nice time?" Helene asked as she kissed me by the front door once again.

"Splendid," I said, feeling exhausted and sweaty.

"Well, that was really quite an honour," Maximilian said as we were riding home.

"Hm?"

"Wolfgang's colleagues. That was quite a display of respect."

"What do you mean?"

"I've never before heard them talk shop like that with a woman. It was as though they took you for one of their own."

For a moment I thought he was joking. Then, to my shock, I realized he meant it in all earnestness.

6 At first I couldn't take Hulda's letter informing me of Leopold's death seriously. This has to be some sort of prank, I thought. Leopold had authorized Hulda to inform everyone it could possibly interest that he had died, just so they could all enjoy the sense of relief when they subsequently found out it was false, and at the same time forgive him for all his offences, both public and private, welcome him back into their lives, and even his most august highness the emperor would have to swallow his obligation to the law and allow Leopold to return to Austria without serving that senseless prison sentence. After all, he can't – a person who was living just yesterday – he can't just up and die without any warning?

I had been present as Sasha was dying. Before my eyes the life left his body, the cruel causality of illness and death unfolding before my eyes and leaving no possibility that this reality could be suppressed. But Leopold had died behind a curtain and so far away that his death could well seem unreal, if you were at all inclined to see it that way. I might have succumbed to denial, if only Hulda's letter hadn't been so strange that by about my tenth reading of it I had to take it as real. What she had written was just all too real. Anyone carrying out a plot would have written differently.

You'll be angry with me, she wrote, *for not having informed you sooner, and it will be hard for you to believe me when I say that I had no ulterior motives for not writing, but I really and truly did not want to burden you. Ten months ago Leopold shut himself away in his study and, aside from Bertha, who brought him hot meals twice every day, he let nobody in to see him from that day forward. Every morning I came and knocked on his door to ask if he was all right, and each time he replied that he was and asked me not to bother him any more that day. I would rather not describe how he looked when, a month into his voluntary confinement, he came out and found me in the kitchen and said that he was ready, that his mind had finally gone soft once and for all, and he begged me on his knees to take him to the asylum before his condition got even worse. I hope you will believe me when I say that I had grave reservations about committing him to an institution, but he refused to be deterred. Once the doctor determined that his condition was probably the result of syphilis and had almost certainly advanced*

beyond the point of any effective treatment, I took him to the asylum.
As I knew would happen, once he was institutionalized things only got
worse. I am so sorry to have to write this, but he succumbed to idiocy, so
utterly and completely that I can't help but say that death came to him
as a merciful release, ending something that had long since ceased being
a life and returning to his body, which had long since ceased serving his
mind, something that in its silence, at least, was reminiscent of dignity.
I know I must sound heartless in writing this, but I believe that if you
had seen him in his last days, you, too, would understand that his death
came as a comfort for all of us.

"Maximilian?"

"Hm?" he replied, as he continued reading his mail across from
me at the table.

"Leopold has died."

"What?"

"Hulda wrote."

I handed him the letter across the table. I needed somebody to
share it with me, to appreciate its authenticity, to bring the whole
matter from the realm of literature into the realm of reality.

"Are you angry?" he asked once he had read it.

"Why?"

"Because she deprived you of the opportunity of paying your
last respects."

I wasn't angry. Remarkably I didn't fault Hulda for anything and
I understood why she had acted as she had. Would I have wanted to
go see Leopold falling apart? Would I have wanted to watch from
close up as his personality disintegrated?

"I don't know," I said, "I suspect not."

I believe that I truly wasn't angry. Nor was I sad. Overall I felt
amazingly little, just as though someone had put a glass vase over
my head or wrapped it in a wet sheet, so that all reality reached me

from a great distance, as though my soul resided somewhere deep, deep down in my body, so far down that it could hardly see out through the long tunnel into which it had dragged itself.

At first I thought it was because I was in shock, but that feeling stayed with me even after any shock should have passed, when I should have proceeded to mourning and begun moving through the pain towards a future in which I would be released from that pain. I asked Maximilian if we could skip the funeral and send Hulda a card of condolences instead. The thought of travelling to Lindheim and back seemed so exhausting and unnecessary that I couldn't even really imagine it, much less carry it out. Maximilian was startled, but put up no resistance. I was grateful to him for that.

On the day of the funeral I woke up without my voice. It's not that I was hoarse, my throat was just fine. It wasn't until Maximilian asked me at breakfast how I had slept that I realized my *fine, thank you* hadn't crossed the threshold of my vocal chords.

"Nada?" Maximilian asked.

I pointed to my throat.

"Have you caught cold?"

I shrugged, even though I knew that I hadn't. It was something else.

"Go back to bed before you make the rest of us ill," he said. "I'll have Ruslana bring your breakfast up to you. All right?"

I dutifully nodded assent. The best thing would be for me to sleep it all off and by the next day everything would be back to normal.

Of course it wasn't. Neither the next day nor the day after that, nor even the following week nor the week after that was I back to speaking again. What if, I started to wonder, my mind has gone soft, too? Without paying any particular attention to the fact that Leopold and I weren't blood relatives, I suddenly became convinced that the mental illness that Hulda believed Leopold had taken with him to the grave was now being carried by me, in my body, into the future. It was obvious – Leopold had died and I promptly went crazy, as though I were obediently ensuring that his legacy did not pass into oblivion. When Maximilian first suggested that we call Wolfgang and ask his opinion about my symptoms, I just reached for a piece of paper and wrote on it *please don't.* I was terrified of being identified as insane, of being committed to an asylum until some day, my mouth foaming, I finally died in a last attempt to avoid any further humiliation.

"Fine," Maximilian said, "let's say I trust you. But I'm worried about you, don't you realize?"

I nodded. He probably really was worried.

One morning I woke up with a sudden insight: I hadn't lost my voice; it was that my body had rejected German. My intellect, within the domain of which all writing resided, my intellect, which was not so sensitive to this necessity, was able to retain traces of that foreign language, but my body had given a clear sign that I had to go back to my real roots. Leopold's death had been a sign that there was no time to waste, that I had to become what he had prophesied I would while he was still living, and how was I supposed to become the liberator of the Slavs if I kept speaking German?

When Ruslana arrived with my breakfast, I already had the first sheet of paper prepared for her.

Ruslana, you have to teach me, it said.

"Teach you what?" she asked, confused.

What, indeed? Ruthenian? Was that what people had begun calling Ukrainian? Russian? Were those even two separate things? Certainly not Polish, that much was clear.

Your language, I wrote.

Ruslana burst out laughing.

"How can I teach you if you can't speak?"

Maybe we could start with writing, I wrote.

"All right," she said in the voice of a strict governess. "We'll begin after dinner."

She seemed to be happy that someone had entrusted her with that responsibility; it did her good to think that someone saw her as capable of more than combing her mistress's hair out and tightening her corset.

After dinner it turned out that I had no talent for learning foreign languages, if only because I lacked the necessary ability to concentrate. I studied Ruslana, noticing how pretty she was when she was focused and strict, as if the satisfaction that trust and respect lent a person could be read from their face. I observed how confidently her hand wrote, how precise her handwriting was, and how mine looked like a five-year-old's by comparison. I studied everything except what I was supposed to be learning. After an hour's practise I knew precisely as much of the Cyrillic alphabet as I had an hour before, but I was convinced that I had learned much that was new about Ruslana.

Shall we review this tomorrow? I wrote at the bottom of my tortured cursive attempts.

"If it would give you pleasure," she said.

I nodded. That was just splendid.

"Does it really seem wise to you to learn the language from a semi-literate housemaid?" Maximilian asked when he came to see how I was doing that evening. "Shouldn't we perhaps hire a proper teacher for you?"

You have no idea how splendid Ruslana is, I wrote.

"If you say so," he said, stroking my cheek. "As long as it makes you happy."

And although I really was happy, I gradually started to grow melancholy. I managed with great effort to learn the Cyrillic alphabet. I could understand simple words like mother and cat. But I hadn't yet begun speaking again. When I realized that I could scarcely remember what my own voice sounded like, the real anxiety set in. If my solution wasn't working, did that mean something else was at work? Was I being punished for something? Or had my very first thought been the most likely explanation, after all, and from one day to the next I really was becoming more and more of an idiot?

Ruslana, there's no point any more, I wrote her after roughly a month.

"Oh, but there is," she said, "look what splendid progress you're making."

Depends how you look at it.

"Forgive me," she said, "I don't mean to interfere, but shouldn't you really contact a doctor about your voice rather than depend on me?"

I waved that away. I would have preferred to stay in bed with no voice than call for a doctor, even if it was Wolfgang. I was much too afraid of what he might tell me.

Why don't you tell me a story instead.

"What kind of story?" she asked.

A story from where you're from.

"I'm afraid," she said hesitantly, "that you have a slightly false notion of what my home is like, if you assume that I could tell you an entertaining story from there."

What sort of notion would be accurate?

"One that assumed a person would need to flee from there to Vienna if they had any hope of not dying from boredom or hunger, even if it meant they would need to be a servant in strangers' houses to the day they died."

"Aren't you homesick at all?" I asked. "Until then I had always assumed as a matter of course that everyone felt about Galicia the way Leopold did."

"Oh, but I am, of course I am," she said. "But that doesn't change anything."

She shook her head, as though that helped her concentrate.

"I'm sorry, I didn't mean to burden you with my problems," she said. "Do you know what we can do? I can sing you a song."

'No, don't,' I was about to say, wanting to spare her from playing the role that I had played so often myself, the role of a dancing circus monkey, go and do something more useful with your time than entertaining me, that was what I wanted to tell her, but I didn't. I said none of those things, because I was too curious.

When Ruslana closed her eyes and began to sing, I didn't really understand what she was singing about. Somewhere the sun was setting and evening approached, perhaps there was a girl sobbing somewhere and perhaps somebody had died, I couldn't quite tell. It was simply the sorrow, as if identical with beauty, the dense sorrow of her voice that uncontrollably flooded the room, and before I knew it I was awash in tears. When she finished and I finally opened my eyes, I realized that her eyes were still shut and her cheeks were now wet.

"I'm sorry," she said when she collected herself, "I didn't mean to make you cry."

My first thought was to reach for the paper, but then I thought of trying to use my voice.

"Please don't apologize," I said, "it was so beautiful."

The words slid through my vocal chords with the same natural force as a torrent over steep cliffs.

"Mrs. Moser!" Ruslana exclaimed. "You've spoken!"

Suddenly she burst into tears again. At that moment I vainly assumed they were tears of compassion, though today I don't know what to think of it all.

I nodded. The worst has passed, I thought to myself. That turned out to be a naive notion, too.

7 Surprisingly, when Anna died, I didn't fall mute. Perhaps because I was too preoccupied with what I was feeling – or rather, not feeling – from the neck down, or perhaps because whatever I was feeling – or rather, not feeling – from the neck down was being felt in my absence. A person, a woman uses the incredible amount of time dedicated to pregnancy to adapt to the being she has become. To reconcile herself with the fact that her belly isn't empty, that there's something in there and that this something is going to be there a long time, that she's going to feel it, and that her body is going to spend a long time being a body in which another body takes shape. A lot of intellectual effort is needed for that new body, which contains yet another, to learn how to view itself as something unified and not something alienated from itself by that change. Perhaps for that reason a person, a woman sees even more clearly that there's nobody who can be close to her in that process of accommodation, who can meet her halfway, simplify anything, bear part of the burden for her. And just when she's learned how to live with that change, the change itself passes. I like to think that mothers who give birth to live children don't notice that second change, because they're preoccupied with the new life that they have to devote themselves to, while I had infinite resources of time and space available to feel to the fullest the void that had taken the place of my pregnancy. But as I said, I didn't fall silent.

I fell silent some six years later, and that time the attack similarly came in the mail. Wanda had written to me. Her lover Armand was dead, and she and Mitja had left Paris to settle in Lausanne. *It's so beautiful*, she wrote. *As beautiful as it was in Bruck. Unadorned nature, devoid of humans, free of catty remarks.* Wanda, whom the world of human things had rewarded with nothing but disillusionment, was able to find beauty only in that which utterly excluded the human.

It was beautiful in Lausanne, and she wanted to stay there. *But a woman, and especially an elderly woman with trembling hands is too clumsy to continue making a living on sewing jobs, a woman who can only live off literature, and for women's literature, such a woman is salaried by no one and can only hope to survive, and Mitja, Mitja has shown no particular talent for making money, and in that respect he resembles Leopold,* she wrote, *but he lacks a title to protect him, now that he's just hers, and with her presenting no value to the world.* Gently but obviously Wanda was testing the depth of my heart, my hospitality. She wasn't asking outright, but the whole letter seemed to be enquiring whether she and Mitja might come lodge with us in Vienna.

"When there's something we don't want," as Freud told me later, "but our moral sense commands us to want it, we'll do everything in our power to prove to ourselves that we truly can't do it. You, for instance, lost the ability to speak."

I'm afraid she'd get in Maximilian's way, I tried to tell myself, keeping the letter a secret from him. I'm afraid, as I tried to tell myself when I allowed myself to venture farther into the matter, that the past would swallow me up if I gave it half a chance, but I kept the most important part of it even from myself. I'm too occupied with my own self, I should have admitted but didn't, to take on the burden of my elderly mother and a brother I scarcely remember. I was selfish, but rather than call myself selfish, I said nothing at all, and preferred to portray my silence as a physical symptom, rather than as the will of my mind. I didn't reply to Wanda's letter. What was still worse, with respect to my turning my back on the woman who had more or less been my mother when she had no one else who could help her, I never really had a bad conscience about it.

And then I woke up with no voice. Something that I had once been able to write off as a peculiar incident now assumed the dimensions of a personal flaw, as something that had no intention of vanishing on its own, as something that might be with me permanently.

I was silent all winter and began to get anxious, while Maximilian grew testy. All the clever excuses for our absence from the social circuit had been exhausted and were now followed by transparent, partial, feeble excuses. I was sleeping poorly and I wished I could close my eyes and wake up healthy, complete and happy, as though nothing were wrong.

All winter long a dense, sticky snow fell, adhering to the ground, and through the window I watched as the city was strangled, swaddled in cotton, isolated, muffled. Would spring even come this year?

"What is the matter?" Maximilian kept asking with inexhaustible persistence.

I don't know, I answered with the same inexhaustible persistence, in a hand that, too big for the tiny sheets of paper it was written on, became more and more like the screams of an enraged child who's bothered by something, though neither he nor his parents can figure out what.

"You need to speak with Wolfgang," he finally said, for at the very least, Wolfgang was family and a highly discreet person.

Life and the prospect of life suddenly seemed more important than shame or pride. I nodded assent. Indeed, I needed to speak with Wolfgang.

But Wolfgang? Wolfgang was a dermatologist and even he didn't know what to do with me.

Had I fallen? Did my neck hurt? My ribcage, my lungs? Had I ever been hoarse before?

He took my pulse, tapped my neck, examined my throat and pronounced it aphonia. Aphonia. The thing had been given its name, but it didn't seem any the more under control for that. "In cases of aphonia," Wolfgang said, "there can sometimes be a nerve that's pinched, or it can be an echo of pneumonia, or it can also be the result of psychosexual trauma, but I, I am no specialist and I recommend a Dr. Freud, who is quite avant-garde in his principles, but a good doctor." If I agreed and if Maximilian did, too, he would arrange a session for me.

"We agree," Maximilian said.

"Most of all," he said as he closed the lid on his briefcase, "you need to spend more time among people. Helene is planning a masquerade ball to mark the arrival of spring. Shall we go?"

"It's ladies' choice," he said, "and till midnight you'll all have to remain in disguise, so a mysterious, silent masked beauty shouldn't strike anyone as anything odd."

"We'll give it some thought," Maximilian said.

It was March and I was still mute. It was the day whenHelene announced her celebration of spring. But outside it was still winter.

"I have a gift for you," Maximilian said and led me by the hand to his bed, where he had set it out on display.

It was a dress for the ball, not entirely green, but definitely not blue, but also not entirely turquoise. It was an Alpine stream and a glass of absinthe and it was a spurious concoction in a chemist's laboratory – it was nature and culture in one and it was quite beautiful.

And with it a mask, one made of metal like the masks behind which a leprous face might be hidden, whose lack of expression conceals our anxiety, the slits for the eyes turned slightly downward, as though expressing sorrow, while the mouth is even and silent. It was terrifying, the mask he had chosen, but it was the mask that I needed. It was the mask that made it possible for me in my muteness to tell the truth of myself, wordlessly and without my having to understand it as a concept; it made it possible for me to express that truth as I felt it without having to give explanations. It was emotion cleansed of all reason. It was as though he knew precisely how I felt, and for the first time. But also the last.

"Silence," Maximilian said as he pointed to it.

I had never before loved him so much as I did at that moment, nor did I afterwards, ever.

"Tell me you'll go," he begged me, "even if just for an hour or so. Just tug my sleeve the instant you want to go home, and we'll go, but tell me you'll go. Surely it can't do any harm."

And indeed, could it be any worse? I nodded assent. I said that I'd go.

The celebration of spring took place as celebrations of spring ought to. It was noisy, it was as though drunken forest sprites were running through the orchard and kissing sleeping shepherds, it was threatening, but even I had to admit that, more than anything else, it was fun. Helene, the only woman who kept her dignity even when she was dressed in yellow, was wearing yellow, her mask was a bird's head and, unaccustomed to the beak, she kissed us with difficulty. Laughing, she ran off like a spring torrent without giving us a minute of her time.

For a long time we stood off to the side. Maximilian criticized people and their clothes and tried to guess from my eyes whether I agreed with him. It was a good game, I found it amusing, and it deprived the people who bumped into us of the power to scare me. And then Maximilian suddenly decided that I needed to dance. Was I a burden to him? His face seemed to be happy.

"Ladies' choice," he said, "I'm dying to know what kind of man you're going to choose."

Was that a trap? His face still seemed to be happy. Under my mask I raised my eyebrows and Maximilian, who could only see my eyes widening into a question, nodded.

I glanced around the room. There was Gustav Klimt, built like a workhorse, disguised as a goat. Or maybe a satyr? Or Satan? Was there any difference? The curls at his temples swept sharply upward, towards his bald head. Wolfgang – considerate, genteel, concerned that all glasses be full and all of the guests happy – if he was wearing a disguise at all, it was so subtle that he looked like he always looked. And then there was a man whom I was seeing for the first time. Tall, his broad shoulders thrust back, with tousled hair, dressed in clothes that looked like an afterthought. Some young Werther? His face was rigid and devoid of all symmetry, his hands were a peasant's, and like his clothes he wore his defects with a kind of taunting arrogance. Distinctive, the gossips would have said. I'd made my choice.

I went over to him and bowed slightly.

He correctly presumed what I wanted and I was grateful to him for sparing me the awkwardness of an explanation that I couldn't have made. He took my hand and we leapt into a waltz.

There's nothing more insipid, I remember thinking, than upbeat music. All music ought to be like Ruslana's songs. All music ought to be sorrow transformed into beauty so that we can bear it more easily. In the course of the waltz even this man, who had tried so hard to seem mysterious, proved to be banal. But he was a good dancer, he knew how to give me leeway and at same time stay in charge, he knew how to lead, but without making me feel led, and he looked me so steadily in the eyes that even I had to focus and forget how much I hated waltzes. I intrigued him, and his interest unlocked mine. Why did I interest him? Was it my silence?

He returned me to Maximilian, offered a deep bow, and vanished. Who on earth was he? I looked at Maximilian and smiled, but the mouth of my rigid mask remained motionless.

"Jakob Frischauer," Maximilian said. "Now and then he writes columns for the *Neue Freie Presse*. A decent choice, I was worried you'd set your sights on Klimt."

His face still appeared to be untroubled.

And then the two of them were suddenly in front of us: Klimt and a forest sprite with the hair of Emilie Flöge, who had latched on to his arm as though his existence depended on her grip and he ran the risk of evaporating into thin air if she let go for an instant. Klimt wasn't wearing a mask, but he was shirtless and naked down to the navel, dressed only in trousers that had been covered with goat fur and a pair of women's pumps that had been deftly refashioned as hooves.

Emilie recognized me in an instant by my hair, as did I her, and she immediately embraced me. Klimt kissed my hand, but his grip was insatiable and I could even feel his hot breath through my glove.

"You must let me sew you something, Nada," Emilie said as she tested the skirt of my dress with her hand. "You're too beautiful to be wearing such provincial kitsch."

Had she meant to be kind but was only cruel by mistake, or had she meant to be cruel but softened her cruelty with the appearance of kindness only out of a sense of proper upbringing? Was she nervous? A river of people carried her away.

I gave Maximilian's sleeve a tug. It's time, was what I wanted to communicate to him with a look. It was almost midnight. He nodded.

"Just let me say some goodbyes," he said. "Will you wait here?"

I nodded and retreated towards the wall, practically crawling under the staircase and hiding in the shadows. I ought to have gone with him, I thought, I would be safest with him. Should I go and find him? But I didn't know which way he had gone, and my burrow seemed so well concealed that I didn't want to give it up, so I stayed there.

And then, suddenly, it was midnight and the masks had been dropped. The whole room was a threat, it suddenly seemed, and each person a spy sent to uncover my secret, my weakness, my infirmity, and how was I to defend myself without any language? Where was Maximilian to protect me, what leave-takings could be occupying him for so long?

As if in a nightmare, there was suddenly a man in front of me, as though he'd sprouted out of the earth, with the obvious intention of talking to me. And it wasn't Maximilian, it was Jakob Frischauer, the man I'd danced with.

"Take the mask off," he said.

That was the rule and there was no cheating on this. I took my mask off, head bowed, eyes fixed on the floor, as though I'd just lost a duel.

"I knew it!" he said. "You are Sacher-Masoch's daughter!" He reached for my hand. "Jakob Frischauer." I didn't feel his kiss through my glove. He was fastidious.

"Is it that obvious?" I said without thinking, spontaneously, as though sneezing. Without any effort, as if speech had always belonged to me, uninterruptedly. I cleared my throat, more out of surprise than necessity. The look on my face must have been one of complete perplexity.

Was it the masquerade? Was it the attention? Was it because he had mentioned Leopold? Or had there perhaps been something about him that had given me my voice back, I later asked Freud. Who's to say, he replied, that every effect has just a single cause?

"I'm sorry?" Jakob said. " I beg your pardon, I didn't hear what you said."

Suddenly I was afraid that I'd only imagined answering him, and was just as mute as before.

"Is it that obvious?" I repeated.

He responded to that and I relaxed. Months of anxiety, months of uncertainty dropped away like an avalanche triggered high in the mountains. In my head there was a vague roaring sound.

"I hope so," he said with a jocular look on his face, or at least that's how it struck me.

"In that case you probably haven't read much of *Psychopatia Sexualis*," I replied half in jest.

"Quite the opposite," he said. "Wasn't it Krafft-Ebing who said that frailties of the body don't diminish greatness of spirit?"

"Apparently you didn't read very carefully," I corrected him. After all, that was my specialty. He said that my father could have laid claim to greatness of spirit, if only he hadn't succumbed to the frailty of his body.

"Still, I owe him a lot."

"Don't we all," I said, as though cracking an off-colour joke.

"You joke, but it took reading your father's *Jewish Stories* to enable me to start relating to myself with something other than disgust."

What candour, I thought. And so young! Aside from Leopold, who made a circus of his shortcomings, I hadn't known many men who could so readily admit to their weaknesses.

At that moment we were approached by a tiny woman in a simple black dress that, judging from the looks of it, had been worn more often than is proper for a person's formal wear. Even her shoes, which were too delicate for the snow cover that still pressed down on the world outside, suggested that her wardrobe boasted at most one other decent pair.

Steering clear of some overly billowy crinolines, she arrived at Jakob's left side and took hold of him by his upper arm, as though declaring proprietorship. They gave each other endearing looks.

They were a couple. Perhaps in love. Or perhaps they did a good job of pretending to be.

"Allow me to introduce you," Jakob said. "This is Rachael, my wife. Rachael, this is Nadezhda von Moser, the daughter of Leopold Sacher-Masoch."

Jakob was one of those rare Viennese who didn't needlessly cling to the wild child myth, even though he had to be aware of it.

Rachael was a fragile brunette with a face that could be both vulnerable and decisive at once. She managed her obvious poverty with a dignity that ruled out anyone's pity. I felt an almost childlike wish for us to become friends.

But it appeared that Rachael was no friend of either change or fun. And she couldn't have cared less whose daughter I was. She wanted to go home.

"Perhaps we could think about heading home," she said to Jakob, to which Jakob nodded.

"It's been a great pleasure," he said in parting.

"For me, as well," I said, nodding my head in a slight bow.

Rachael said nothing.

"May I ask," Freud asked me once, "why it was that you seduced the husband of the first woman who interested you enough for you to want to have her as your friend?"

"Does a woman enter into a relationship with a man on account of his wife?" I asked.

"Sometimes," Freud said.

I was silent for a time, then I remembered Kathrin.

For a short time Leopold and Wanda had been friends with Kathrin Strebinger who took the peculiar stance of seducing the husband of every woman who maintained she was happily married. "There are no happily married women," she claimed. And it was better for them to find that out too soon rather than too late.

"Did she seduce your father?" Freud asked.

"No," I replied. "Wanda never lied about being happily married. And Leopold was repulsed by assertive women."

It wasn't until I had said that out loud that I realized it was true. Leopold was fond of lying that he was fascinated by feminine power, but in fact he couldn't bear having anyone set the pace but himself. He was interested in women who were willing to wear furs and wield a whip only when he was issuing the orders.

"What part of your story reminded you of Kathrin Strebinger? Did you want to protect Rachael from her husband?"

"No, there was nothing," I said. "Your assumption reminded me of her. Jakob Frischauer was a decent person."

"Even though he was pathologically unfaithful, and you faulted your father above all for his unfaithfulness?"

This left me silent for a long time, until I said: "I fell in love with him. I seduced him because I'd fallen in love with him."

"Did you wait until the day you could be certain he would never become part of your life to fall in love with him?"

The admission that I had in fact been in love with Jakob was so undeniable for me that I couldn't bear having anyone dispute it. Sometimes Freud could be so tacky, so convinced of his own infallibility.

"Sometimes I get the impression," I said, "that you make claims simply in order to maintain the impression that you're always right, as opposed to your patients."

"Your resistance can be quite vehement."

"Well what about yours?" I asked. "How vehement must your resistance be that you begrudge me even the most fundamental validation for telling the truth?"

"I'm convinced," Freud said, "that you believe you're telling the truth."

"And I'm convinced," I said getting up off the couch, "that we're finished for today."

"For today," Freud said, watching my departure with his arms crossed.

"Frischauer," Maximilian assured me without any doubt as we were walking home, "is one of those people who have to tell everyone that they're Jews, so that nobody suspects they're responsible for their failure themselves.

"He lacks nothing," he said. "He could at least have enough pride not to market himself as a victim and tend to his work, instead. Of course he's constantly facing down poverty, considering he writes for the feuilletons at most twice a year."

At that instant I recalled with painful clarity all the ladies who stumbled their way through the syllables of my last name without betraying the slightest self-consciousness; the sincerity with which Emilie Flöge had made fun of my countrified manners; the flippant conversations about Leopold's perversions that would unfold in serene disregard of my presence and during which I would say nothing. Poor Maximilian, there was no way he could understand, natural born insider that he was.

"I understand," I said without a trace of understanding in my voice.

Abruptly Maximilian turned around and looked at me from one side.

"Nada!"

"Yes? "

"You're talking!"

I smiled and nodded. Whatever it was that had come over me seemed to be gone. Let's hope forever, I thought. Let's not ever go back there again.

"I know," I said.

Maximilian embraced me with both arms and hugged me so tight that I tumbled into his embrace and banged the crown of my head against his chin.

"Didn't I tell you that you needed to get out and around more."

8 I had never seen the office of the old chief of police in Lemberg, but when I saw Freud's consulting room the perception that there was a likeness between the two places arose like a ghost in my consciousness.

Leopold rarely mentioned his father, and when he did, it was with a sort of forced reverence. Only once, when he was ill, did he permit himself a slip of the truth. It was when he had pneumonia, and I was sitting at his bedside, changing the wet compresses on his forehead.

"Is it possible," he suddenly said with no warning, "that on the day your father died you were happy? Were you happy because he was dead?"

He looked at me feverishly, and although it was as if there was a film over his eyes, they singled me out so emphatically that it took a lot of energy from me. His sweaty hand grabbed me by the wrist.

"Are you also going to be happy when I die?"

I was seven years old and didn't understand. Him, his illness, his guilt, his projection. I was frightened. I shook my head too energetically, nearly breaking my neck, but Leopold appeared to be comforted. He closed his eyes and dropped off to sleep.

After that he spoke even more seldom about his father. I'm almost certain that he never described him – neither his manner of dress, nor his build and face, nor his behaviour, beliefs and principles. Everything I knew about him – about that person who died before I even had a chance to know him – I had to intuit from Leopold's personality and his description of his father's office.

Perhaps that's why my image of him was so deeply imprinted on my mind. His herb garden, the butterflies affixed with pins to their spots in the glass-covered cases, the marionette in the likeness of a Carpathian robber standing obediently in the corner, subdued for all time.

He must have loved order, old Sacher-Masoch, he must have been domineeringly rational, that botanist, that collector of crystals, tusks and bones. Even in his godlessness he must have been unwaveringly convinced that man was destined to rule the earth by breaking it down into smaller categories to be sorted and named. The selection of portrait busts arranged on the desk in front of him attested to his models: Frederick the Great, Napoleon, Socrates, Goethe. Bear skins were arrayed along the walls as durable evidence of his hunting exploits. He was the lord of the law, the hand of reason, set down in that uneasy province beset by outright beastly passions in order to rule it. Old Sacher-Moser must have been everything that Leopold was not. Reliable, pedantic, and conscientious, if domineering, unrelenting and cruel, but above all he had to be exalted. A man whom the fact that nobody contradicted him solidified in the conviction that doubt was something that only afflicted others.

Even Freud, if you could judge him by the state of his office, was different in every respect from old Sacher-Moser, but because he wasn't his son, he could be different without defying him. He was a collector, too, but what he collected was already named. Freud's collection consisted of things that stood in for what surpassed human beings, not what humans were able to dominate. His office desk was cluttered with figurines of wise men, gods, and beasts that were never meant to be merely beasts. Pallas Athena, a Chinese sage, Isis with Horus in her lap, one of Toto's baboons, statuettes vainly announcing what kind of company Freud would have chosen if he could choose. They represented the community that he wanted to be a member of, and in this respect they expressed his arrogance as well as his doubt. They were turned to face him, not the patient. If old Sacher-Masoch's collection signified that he wanted followers, Freud's testified to a need for companions. Was he lonely?

If Wolfgang was a physician, Freud had to be something different. There was nothing clinical about his appearance, and although he liked to use phrases that were typical for his field, the sentences had the shape of philosophy. It was strange listening to him. He talked like Leopold, except that you got no sense from his words that they were driven by anything personal, and even his behaviour didn't by any means point towards the instability that I had associated until then with that manner of speaking. If, up until then, I had known only men who represented order and men who represented chaos, Freud gave the impression of someone who was trying to balance the two. Within the space of a single sentence he was likely to veer from a casual tone to a solemn one at least twice, only to end up on a high note. I couldn't help but think of Jakob Frischauer. Was he like this, too? Did I want him to be?

I liked the man – Freud – when he shook my hand, firmly but cautiously. He was ever so slightly cross-eyed, and his tight vest and plump fingers suggested he could easily become overweight, but so far had managed to avoid that. I liked him, although I had come there to let him know that I didn't really need to come.

"Have a seat," he said.

My memory has dutifully managed to misplace the memory of how I described my experience of aphonia when he asked me about it. During the years when it wasn't yet fixed, my misappropriation of the memory had faded until it finally disappeared altogether. What remained was the memory of an authentic experience. Of something physical that wasn't pain, but also wasn't the silence of sobbing, a lump of remorse that words couldn't penetrate. A memory of the throat at war with its vocal chords. And a memory of Freud's mistrust.

"A person who lies," Freud said, "always talks about events as though they hadn't happened to him. As though he were writing a novel, if you know what I mean, and not a particularly good one, at that. He'll speak as though he's describing a protagonist under duress, but in such a way that the drama of it all is trapped at the level of words and sentences, without any connection to the depths they represent. Even when he talks in the first person, which is rare, it will feel as though he's talking about some third person, because the emotions that accompany authentic experiences will be missing. A person who's telling the truth will always seem just a shade embarrassed."

"Thank you," I said. "Now I know what narrative forms to avoid if I ever want to lie to you."

"You're clever," Freud said. "But the cleverest patients are usually the ones who are the most stubbornly defensive of their illness. Out of vanity."

"I'm not ill any more," I repeated.

I didn't feel ill. On the contrary, for the first time in a long time I felt as though I didn't have to fight for the will to live, as though it had been served up to me, ready-made and ready to wear. As though my breasts were full of springtime, as though dried branches had sprouted meaty buds, ready to burgeon into lush foliage. If I start devoting myself to that illness, I told myself, I may be forced to give up this joy, and I wanted to avoid that at any cost. It was too precious, too rare.

"As you wish, Mrs. Moser," Freud said, smiling. "It's pointless to try to cure a patient against their will."

I nodded and slowly rose from my chair.

"But what if, let's say, the condition comes back..." I said, only half standing, unsure of what I really wanted.

"If it comes back, I advise you to contact me immediately."

"But let's say it recurs in some milder form, as hoarseness, or a cold. Could you prescribe something to get it under control?"

"I would prefer that you contact me rather than try to self-diagnose and treat yourself."

"Of course," I replied. "But still, in case of an emergency."

"I can write you a prescription for heroin."

"I beg your pardon," I said. "I'm not familiar with it."

I raised my eyebrows.

"Oh, those Bavarians have come up with another universal remedy for everything from a cough to a migraine. Something like morphine, except that it's not habit-forming, supposedly," he said, not convinced.

"Will it help?"

"Almost certainly not. But it will almost certainly give you the feeling that you've done something for yourself, without having actually done anything for yourself at all."

"In that case, yes, please write me a prescription," I laughed.

"You're quite witty," he said, and considering the warning he'd just given me, it was hard to determine whether that was meant as a compliment or a reproach. "Still, if you have any similar attacks, please contact me. I know that the thought of needing help is offensive, but it shouldn't be. A person who's trying to rid himself of his weaknesses has nothing to be ashamed of. Quite the contrary, it's the person who stubbornly insists on his rights, no matter how much he injures himself and those forced to live with him, who ought to be ashamed."

I knew what he was talking about, and he was right. Wasn't that precisely what I had most stubbornly faulted Leopold for? His bullish refusal to make peace with his demons? Hadn't I spent my entire childhood trying to understand why somebody would insist so stubbornly on being ill? But I felt so happy and healthy and it was as though his words had no bearing on me.

"Of course," I said, as I brought the slow process of getting up to a close, offered him a negligent handshake good-bye and dispersed through the front door of Berggasse 19 into the spring fog. I didn't try to determine if he was watching me leave. I couldn't have cared less.

Evening came on, and the sky over the rooftops took on a pinkish hue and the wind, although still chilly, bore the faint olfactory promise of spring. There was nobody in my life who believed, there were no fatalists, and even I myself always believed there was something vaguely tasteless about the way people pushed the responsibility for their own actions off on to external forces. But sometimes, if rarely, I still wonder if maybe it isn't precisely the most imperceptible factors that predispose a person to a particular decision. Do we commit suicide on account of the weather? Does it make us fall in love? Would my life be totally different if at the time it hadn't been spring?

I took a long time getting home as I lost myself in the beauty, and though we had no agreement about getting home by a certain time, Maximilian was waiting for me at the door with a reproach for getting home late.

During supper he asked about Freud, about our session and his method, and although as a trained lawyer he couldn't have had too clear a notion what medicine was, it didn't take him much effort to conclude that free association didn't qualify.

"To think of all the things people call science these days," Maximilian said, just before stuffing potatoes into the puckered mouth that bafflement left on his face.

To all appearances he approved of my decision not to get treatment, while I for the first time began to appreciate how much I liked

Freud. Maximilian's response distressed me more than I'd expected, and perhaps more than it really needed to do. If he could speak disparagingly of someone I'd decided to praise, was he necessarily disparaging me, too? Did this person from the far side of the roast, my husband, really despise me without even realizing it? The happiness that I'd so zealously protected from Freud was going to hell in a handbasket here without him having to lift a finger.

The more I think about it, the more likely it seems that this was the point at which I decided I needed to write to Jakob, even though I put off actually doing it for some time.

9 For ages Maximilian had made me gifts of the wrong kinds of books.

"Nada is such an avid reader," he would occasionally tell someone, and he was right. I was an avid reader.

Wanda was an avid reader. Wanda had to read to keep from hanging herself, from opening an artery with a letter opener, from borrowing a hunting rifle and shooting herself in the head, she occasionally said. She was one of those people who, the older she got, didn't look back on her childhood with increasing nostalgia.

"My father was a womanizer", she would say. "If I came home too early from school, I might find some syphilitic whore lying in my mother's bed.

"Mother and I would sew gloves to survive, in a dimly lit, unheated apartment.

"Whenever I went without food for too long, I would peer in through the display window of the bakery, as if the sight of bread could still the hunger pangs."

When Wanda talked about her childhood, it was as though she were reading from a novel by Émile Zola. Her descriptions were so dry and devoid of ornamentation that you knew they had to be true. Wanda had to read if she wanted to believe that there was some other way of life besides poverty. Of course she fell in love with a writer.

Reading, Wanda had taught me, was a way of escaping from life. There was nothing about my straitened circumstances that resembled hers, and yet I was also intent on something similar. Reading, I had found out on my own, was like having a life and not having one, like living without having to risk anything, it was easy and felt liberating, even though it didn't leave you with anything tangible.

Maximilian was aware of my passion and for a long time I thought it suited him. My reading habits provided a nice counterpart to the image he'd formed of me before really getting to know me, the image of the wild woman from the east who mustered all the unbridled force that she'd inherited from nature, yet at the same time was interested in intellectual issues without having to be coerced and was sufficiently capable of refinement that you could take her out and show her around.

At first his gifts reinforced my conviction, despite their inappropriateness. Maximilian is just trying to be nice, I thought for the longest time, it's just that he's superficial. For instance, when Ruslana and I started practising the Cyrillic alphabet after my first attack of aphonia, he made me a gift of Sienkiewicz's *With Fire and Sword*.

Thank you, I wrote to him, making a point of writing it in Cyrillic, and gave him a kiss on the cheek. I remembered Leopold, I remembered how he could look at Wanda with such disdain whenever she referred to his habits or style as "Polish". His pan-Slavism, which was shallow enough as it was, had never made any provision for including Poles in the new, shared Slavic homeland. In his eyes all Poles were exemplified by the tale of the Galician nobleman who would summon his serfs and their wives before him, whole villages at a time, order the wives to hike their skirts up over their heads until they were standing before him naked from the waist down, and then order the peasants to find their wives from behind. Whichever of them didn't get it right was first given fifty lashes and then impaled. Was there something distinctively Polish about his cruelty? Surely not, but regardless of how unfair he could be, I had inherited Leopold's revulsion in its entirety and would also roll my eyes whenever Wanda referred to him as a Pole to some visitor. But while Wanda was a poorly educated seamstress who probably would have died of tuberculosis in some alley at the age of twenty, if only an aristocrat of a questionable bent hadn't fallen in love with her, Maximilian saw himself as an educated person and was certainly no ignoramus. He was just inattentive. At a time when I was neurotically gasping for traces of my Ruthenian roots as though my life depended on it, he gave me a freshly plucked flower of Polish nationalism. I'm sure he meant well, I kept telling myself.

Until one day he made me a gift of *Madame Bovary*. First I read it carefully all the way through. And then I began to wonder. I would reread it all night long before finally dropping off towards morning, then waking up an hour later, feverish and moody.

Madame Bovary was the kind of book that Hulda might have written. She had always understood that every woman comes equipped with a kind of inborn pragmatism, which those who wish to live a long and happy life need to cultivate. In other words, she would have been utterly lost amidst a forest of abstractions. The realm of the intellect belonged to men, who knew how to give their imagination free rein to find its limits without straying into the darkness. Not so women – they were too much like animals to be able to control their desire, so the best thing for them was to forget about it entirely. That's why they couldn't be trusted with philosophy or literature, let alone love. A woman who liked to read, *Madame Bovary* taught me, as though mimicking Hulda, was a doomed woman. A woman who read, or a woman who loved, or whatever, was a sentimental woman, and no man was prepared to love a sentimental woman. And an unloved woman, as we knew, couldn't survive.

"Just look at what happened to poor Wanda," Hulda was fond of remarking, as though she'd had no role in what happened to Wanda. "Just look at what happens to a crazy woman who insists that desire counts for something in marriage."

"Did I want to end up like her?" she sometimes asked me.

"Of course not," I would say.

And indeed, I would think to myself, I didn't. But I also didn't want to end up like Hulda. I wanted to believe there was a third way. That a woman could allow herself a thousand lovers and a thousand books without having to organize them around her sentimental hunger for love, and that a predilection for literature, much less a passion for seduction, was anything but a portent of doom.

At breakfast Maximilian informed me that Adele Bloch-Bauer was organizing a wedding party for Alma and Gustav Mahler and that Helene thought it was going to be the social event of the year and we absolutely had to attend.

"Would you want to go?" he asked.

"Why not?"

"Wonderful," he said, biting into a croissant.

I watched in silence as he ate, the crumbs dropping from his fingers onto his plate, the greedy gulps of coffee leaving a white button of foam from the cream on the tip of his nose, the way he immersed himself in his task, his breakfast, his marriage, his life – surely he hadn't given me *Madame Bovary* as a warning? Had he even read it himself?

"Every war has its reasons," Freud said when I asked him for his opinion, "which are complex, carefully concealed, and many." The apparent causes themselves assemble around them rather haphazardly, along the lines of first come, first served. Whenever you want something, and particularly when you wish for something destructive, it can seem as though everything in the world is encouraging you in that direction. Even something as irrelevant as *Madame Bovary*.

Like the house where Helene and Wolfgang lived, the Bloch-Bauers' residence was more of a depot than a home, intended more for public use than for private life. But if Helene's sense of decor gave her guests the feeling that even the furniture couldn't wait for their visit, the Bloch-Bauers' gold- and marble-clad interior had more of an imposing than a welcoming effect. It seemed like a faithful reflection of the inner world of its investor, Ferdinand Bloch-Bauer, who, leaning, or rather sprawled against the fireplace mantelpiece, even while engaged in a seemingly relaxed conversation gave the impression that, in some opera based on motifs from Galician folk tales, he could very well assume the role of the Polish aristocrat from Leopold's nightmares.

At the door the newly-wed Mahlers welcomed the guests, along with their kisses, congratulations and good wishes both feigned and sincere. Alma gave the impression of caring more about the attention being lavished on her than on her husband, while Gustav looked ready to sink into his unease and disappear altogether. I gave him more of a hug than was called for by etiquette. I felt bad for him, because I knew how he felt.

I soon realized that I didn't care much for society and even less for small talk – so what on earth had made me want to come here? Was there nothing else with which I could divert myself? I had expected the social event of the year to amount to more than polite chit-chat. Did I think I would suddenly be able to look at people with more trust? Give them the benefit of the doubt? Want to believe that they were capable of being attentive, understanding, that they weren't just waiting for their chance to jump in? Did I have reasons that I'd managed to hide even from myself? Had I hoped I might by chance run into Jakob? I glanced around the room. Adele Bloch-Bauer was disappearing with Klimt up the stairs. Helene was explaining to Koloman Moser that it was worth it for him to give her the set of chairs she'd fallen in love with just for the sake of the name recognition.

"The name you so easily gave up?" Moser said in jest.

"What doesn't a woman give up for love?" Helene insouciantly replied, even though there was nothing light-hearted about what she said.

"You could always have chosen a husband who would have allowed you to keep your name."

"How could I have known," Helene said, "what a marvellous artist you'd become."

"And besides," Moser said, apparently without any bitterness, "what business does a lady like you have with the son of a caretaker."

"What kind of woman do you take me for?" Helene said in mock indignation.

"Helene," Moser said, gently taking her by the arm, "you know perfectly well it's impossible to blame you for anything."

It was a vicious insult, yet true at the same time. Helene was the kind of person that criticism bounced off. She could have opened a brothel, if she'd wanted, and everyone would have lavished praise on the way she was looking after her girls; factory workers endured far worse conditions, they would have said, finding some prize to award her. She was sweet and endearing, and as a result everything about her seemed marvellous.

"I'm going to go for a walk," I told Maximilian.

He nodded absent-mindedly and I went. On my way I took a glass of champagne from a footman's tray.

The more I circulated among the guests, the more obvious it became I was looking for someone. Where could he be? I wondered. Had he not been invited? Was he not fond of parties? Was he ill? Perhaps he'd come later; it was still early. And if he did come, what was I supposed to do with him? Why had I suddenly, practically behind my own back, wanted Jakob to be here so much, someone I'd barely encountered, a person I knew only as a pair of arms that had guided me through the forced gaiety of a waltz, as a couple of comments that concealed more than they had revealed, despite their apparent frankness, that person whom I knew so little as to not know at all? Why did I want to get to know him better? With a barely conscious wave of the hand I replaced my empty glass with a full one.

Then I noticed her. Sitting on the edge of a sofa, holding a glass in her trembling hands, eyes flitting about the room was Emilie Flöge. Her body language was crying out for attention. How awful it must be that this woman, despite her self-confidence verging on arrogance, couldn't muster enough strength to conceal her anguish. By comparison Mahler seemed to be having a wonderful time. I was on the verge of calling for Helene to come over, but reconsidered.

I sat down next to her. We weren't friends, but there was something about her nervousness, about her chapped lips and chain smoking that shifted my empathy for her towards friendship. I placed a hand on her back and gave her a kiss on the cheek. It would have been stupid to ask what was wrong. All of Vienna knew what was wrong. And again I could see Klimt following Adele Bloch-Bauer up the stairs, slowly, always a step behind her, always at enough of a distance so he could imagine her naked. How was it possible that this man, who so evidently cherished beauty, could behave so vilely towards the people he should have protected, even if that meant protecting them from himself?

"Tell me everything," I said.

"Oh, what is there to say?"

She drew on her cigarette, washing the smoke down with a drink of champagne.

"Women," I said, "should never yield their advantage to men. You should think about taking a new lover. It's long overdue."

What authority I spoke with, I, who for ten years now had been stubbornly avoiding life like the plague, like a threat, like a hazard, I, aged almost thirty, who had never known anything about anything!

Yet Emilie, who couldn't have fathomed the depths of my ignorance, who at that moment, even if she'd wanted to, couldn't have fathomed anything but the depth of her own sorrow, which didn't spill forth in anger only because of the tenacity of her love, just looked at me trustingly and leaned her head on my shoulder. It was as though she was happy that somebody had rescued her from drowning by pulling her on to dry land.

"What good would it do me," she said looking straight ahead, "if I'm not interested in other men. Revenge? Satisfaction?"

I did not contradict her. It was obvious that no advice, no matter how reasonable it might be, was going to change anything. It would have been harder for her to survive without the love that she'd come to identify with herself, than without the pain. Her sorrow could almost have become mine, it was so difficult to see her so submerged in that love that was forever condemned to remain unfairly distributed.

"It might be worth giving some thought," Freud told me at one point, "to why you're so consumed with the fate of Emilie Flöge."

"It sounds to me," I replied, "as though you've already given it some thought."

"She's like you," Freud said.

"Emilie? Because she's a redhead with a mannish face?"

"If you describe her the way you describe yourself," Freud said laughing, "you obviously think that she's like you. You see yourself in her, and in her fate you see the fate of your mother. Or rather, in her you see yourself becoming your mother."

"Emilie's fate doesn't resemble Wanda's in any way," I said. "Emilie has enough money to stay unhappily in love to the day she dies without putting her life in the slightest jeopardy."

"For you," Freud said, "Emilie Flöge is a woman whose life has passed at a pace dictated by a man. Emilie Flöge is your worst nightmare come to life."

Isn't every person always his own worst nightmare come to life? I wondered, but didn't say anything.

10

I wrote to Jakob as though I were alone in the world, as though there was nobody to have to think of aside from myself, not even Jakob, nobody I had to protect from my own capriciousness, I wrote to him with a childish recklessness mixed with the premeditation of someone who had been able to observe people for some time and who knew what to count on from them. I wrote to him inspired by an ineffable sense of confidence and certainty that what I was doing was somehow related to necessity, which by definition meant it couldn't be wrong. This is my first act of free will, I thought to myself as I reached for the pen. Years later Freud smiled at that; his smile was kind, but it was also patronizing and not entirely devoid of irony.

I had lived long enough with Leopold to know how far flattery could get you with men. Tell him "I've heard what you've said and I'm all ears." Tell him he's wise and kind in his wisdom. That there's nobody like him. Tell him that history is saving a place for him. Tell it to him with your body in a way that reinforces your voice. Tell it to him so he believes.

And he believed, dear Jakob, when I told him that although I tried not to, I often thought of him. And indeed, there were grounds for believing. With respect to the content, I didn't lie. I liked him and wished with all my heart for him to be as good as I anticipated he might be. But aside from that, I lied in my method. I made no confessions, I wasn't trusting and open; I was approaching him tactically. And my tactics were good. Practically the next day dear Jakob and I were sitting in the Café Central, as though we were the only two people in the world, as though there were nobody to have to think of but us, and nobody to protect from our caprice.

"You have no idea how hard it is to find a woman who doesn't expect a man to do everything himself," Jakob said in high spirits as he joined me. His hair was wet from the spring shower outside and had curled slightly from the dampness.

"I suppose you blame women for that," I said. You asked for that answer, I thought. Praise your neighbour for her intemperance, but don't be surprised if she then serves it back up to you richly and often.

"Of course not," he said. "I blame their upbringing. In spite of it all, it's nice to meet one who didn't succumb to it."

Oh, there was nothing to succumb to. Everyone in our household had far better things to busy themselves with than manners.

"You must tell me everything about your household," he said. His initial high spirits had solidified into satisfaction: he was satisfied with his decision to come, satisfied that our conversation, barely three minutes old and already so promising in its setting, had developed the way he had planned. I was – or at least so it seemed – exactly what he'd expected of me, what he'd hoped for, perhaps even what he'd dreamed of. This was something new, for I hadn't known until then that I was what I turned out to be in the Café Central that morning, that the thought of sitting there with a stranger, half-obscured in the shade of a marble column, would lift my spirits so much, that the thought of me, a married woman, sitting with him, prevented only by my steel-bone corset from melting into a puddle of excitement, would lift my spirits so much. I hadn't realized that that's what I was, and perhaps to that very day I wasn't, perhaps love was what changed me. Or perhaps love opened the door to something that had been latent in me all along, but hadn't yet had the opportunity to blossom. Whatever it did, it was there, love. It was something new, so I didn't recognize it at first. It was simply the wish to sit differently. The wish to understand every sentence, every thought, as if it were precious. To understand this person whose knee was constantly fidgeting under the table, better than he understood himself. It was the thought that suggested that whatever this was, I had most certainly never felt it towards Maximilian, and that this was what I'd been missing without even realizing it.

"You're lost in thought," Jakob said.

I shook my head. "I'm looking at your knee," I said. "Are you nervous?"

He laughed, as though it made him particularly happy that I'd discovered something about him, as though that meant I was paying closer attention to him than he'd dared to hope for, and indeed I was watching him attentively, I was watching as though every detail about him was particularly crucial, as though it was going to justify my unjustifiable affection for this person I scarcely knew well enough to trust, much less respect.

"Aren't you?" he asked.

That's funny, I thought. I'm not. Why wasn't I nervous? Why wasn't I afraid of the novelty, risk, uncertainty? Why had I walked into this as though I were meeting my fate?

"Should I be?"

"Well, everyone's knees can get just a little weak when they're looking death in the face," he said.

"You're trying to distract me," I said.

"I see you know something about human nature."

"Other people's, sure," I laughed.

"Don't you have anyone to focus on yours? A spiritual mentor?"

I thought of Freud and shook my head. Maximilian didn't even come into question.

"No, no one," I said. "It's all up to me."

He took my by the hand, as though getting ready to promise me something.

"I'll focus on it, if you'll let me."

"First you're going to have to stop your knee fidgeting, and then I can trust you," I said with feigned sagacity, but my hand, which without my permission was holding his, announced that trust had already been granted.

"A small price to pay," he said, forcing his nerves to calm down, as though obeying an order, but only outwardly and only because he didn't want to risk any punishment.

"Not like this," I said. Indeed. It was downright funny to see how our meeting still gave the impression that I was leading, that I was deciding whether there was any pretext for carrying on, as though I were awarding or denying clemency and he was simply going with the flow of my judgement.

"This could take a bit longer," he said.

"But we have time, don't we?"

"As much as you want." He squeezed my hand again. The contact between two hands is so slight, barely taking in any body at all, but when it's forced to carry the entire burden of intimacy, it seems to take in everything, not just the whole body, but the whole spirit as well and everything else that you can't ascribe to just one or the other.

So what else is going to happen now? I wondered.

"Hey, Frischauer!" a voice called out from behind us, as if descending into the undergrowth from the overstory above. It was a deep male voice, well suited to the long, black beard from which it originated.

"Herzl," Jakob said, giving a slight bow of his head. There was something bitter in his voice and his body grew taut as it feigned a relaxed pose. He hasn't let go of my hand, I thought. How nice that he hasn't let go of my hand. How nice that he wants to let the world know that we belong to each other. "I didn't know you were in Vienna," he said. "Hasn't the sultan sliced off part of his empire for your promised land yet?"

He became like a hunting dog flinging itself at a rabbit hutch, Jakob did, when he was put out of sorts. Something was wrong, he wasn't happy to see this man standing tanned and tired before him. This is what you're like when you're upset, I thought. When you're in love with someone, even things about him that ought to put you off seem endearing.

"Frischauer, I didn't come over to bicker with you. I came over to say hello. I wouldn't want us to be enemies."

"And you wouldn't want to give up your dream of a Greater Israel, either, now would you?"

The man in front of us closed his eyes for a moment. This was not the first time he was having this conversation. When he opened them, he looked at me.

"Bring him to his senses, would you?"

This man connects us, I realized and a warm feeling coursed through me at the thought of it. When he looks at us, his linguistic mind processes us not as two separate singular subjects, but as a single dual subject. He thinks I have some influence over Jakob. That I'm someone who, if I cared to, could bring him to his senses.

I smiled kindly.

"And who's going to bring you to your senses, Herzl?" Jakob said.

"It's all right," the man said. "Till we meet again."

He nodded in farewell and left. Next to me I felt Jakob's body relax. Beneath the table his knee started bouncing again.

"That nice man made you nervous?"

"That nice man would like to become a dictator," Jakob said, "but he'd also like the world not to begrudge him that."

"It's hard to believe."

"Just read *The Jewish State* sometime. He's been roaming the world for years trying to wrangle some clump of earth to rule over."

"So the thought of my influence means nothing to you?"

"Would you like me to tell you the whole story, or would you rather make fun of me?"

"I'm listening," I said. "I'm listening. And I'll continue to listen." Now I wasn't approaching him tactically. Now I was simply devoted.

"Herzl was like an older brother to me when I first came to the *Neue Freie Presse* and told them I wanted to write. He knew what it was like for me, what bog of self-doubt I had to gnaw my way through each time I needed to write a declarative sentence, how worthless and ignorant I felt I was, what envy I was filled with at the very sight of those bold young Austrians whose very surnames spared them the least bit of doubt or shame."

At that point I thought I could sense the vast well of tenderness I felt for him moving within me, because I understood the anxiety he told me about so well that I fell in love with him more than I'd ever fallen in love with Maximilian, if not because he was the better person, then simply because he was so very much like me, because the pain he felt at not belonging was so much in accord with my own, although now I think that I simply grasped at it, as though I'd been waiting from the moment I met him for something that would lend some substance to my attraction. I listened to him attentively and devotedly, but more than listening, I looked at him. His firm cheekbones, his hands of a manual labourer. His words were helpful for the way they completed the picture.

"Herzl understood me. Like me, he'd spent most of his youth trying to conceal his Jewishness, but the more he tried to pass himself off as Austrian, the more the Austrians made it clear to him that he didn't fool anyone. I grasped at his understanding, because until then I'd had nobody willing to reassure me that I was smart and talented and how much of a shame it would be if I didn't persist.

"You can't imagine how difficult it is to resist persistent flattery."

"Of course I can imagine. Have you forgotten that I lived with a writer?"

"That must have been a wonderful life," he said without irony.

"Think twice before you wish it on yourself," I said. I was prepared to tell him everything about that life if he wanted to listen, but he didn't seize the opportunity. He was engrossed in his own story and it was important to him that I hear it to the end.

"Your father understood things that Herzl will never be capable of understanding. Do you recall that he served as a correspondent from Paris a good many years ago?"

I didn't.

"I think his career finally took off when he reported on the Dreyfus affair. Suddenly he was convinced that the Jews would only be able to live in peace if they got their own state. As though he didn't understand that, as long as there continued to be states, there would never be peace anywhere. Don't you see, this is what your father understood."

"Sure, at least in principle. Leopold was fond of declaring himself a socialist internationalist, although that didn't keep him from recalling repeatedly how marvellous Austria was and how backward the Germans and Poles were."

"Of course he did," Jakob said, as if it was a given that a man's published articles were a more dependable barometer of his nature than what he'd said. "He understood how ridiculous it was to be proud of something as insubstantial as a nation."

Aside from the fact that he idealized the Ukrainians, I thought, but refrained from saying anything.

"But then Herzl," Jakob said, "Herzl thinks that the Jews can only overcome centuries of persecution by starting to blabber about their cultural greatness and keep babbling until someone believes them."

I noticed how he had used "them". Not "us".

"What do you think?" I asked.

"That a history of eking out a living in other people's countries should have taught us how brutal nations become when they finally gnaw their way through to their own state. And that we shouldn't dare to wish to become brutal ourselves. We should be helping others come to their senses. Help them realize that the land doesn't belong to…"

"But people like to belong to the land," I said. "And they get depressed when they don't."

"Only when they don't have anything genuine keeping them happy."

Was he right?

"How did the two of you fall out? You and Herzl, I mean?"

"He was organizing a congress of Zionists, and I told him that I didn't want to have anything to do with nationalists."

"Do you miss him sometimes?"

"The way he used to be. I prefer not to run into him the way he is now."

I remember how he fell silent after that and only after a pause asked, "What about you? Is there anybody you miss?"

"No, nobody," I said. Yet, I thought.

"You need to get home, before they start missing you."

"You're right."

I got up slowly, as though even my body wasn't keen on leaving. Jakob got up, and for a moment I thought he was going to kiss my hand, but he just reached a hand out to shake, like one man to another. I wished I could interpret the gesture as a sign of respect. Then he bent down towards my ear.

"I'd like to kiss you," he said.

Well, go ahead, I thought.

"But I won't," he said.

Then he sat back down.

As I left, all I could think about was how much I wanted him to follow me with his eyes all the way to the point where I disappeared out the door, but nothing in the world could have brought me to turn back and look.

11 "You didn't sleep well," Maximilian said, kissing me on the forehead before sitting down to breakfast. By then Maximilian and I had spent some seven uninterrupted years sleeping in separate bedrooms. He must have heard me pacing up and down the hallway. Had he had a sleepless night, too?

"There was a full moon," I said.

"I didn't realize," he said, fully aware of the fact that I put no stock in superstitions, "that you put such stock in superstitions."

Maximilian never believed me when I lied, but he never asked any probing questions, either. The truth didn't concern him. Surely it's benign, he thought. Sometimes in company he might even mention to someone that he felt that marriage depended on trust, not on sincerity. Don't you agree, he would turn and rhetorically ask me if we happened to be standing together on those occasions, don't you think so, too, Nada? He liked thinking that the two of us had come to the same conclusion together, even though we'd never had an actual discussion on the subject before. After all, the social contract was never formally approved, either, and yet it still holds, he probably thought. Maximilian was still fond of introducing himself in society as a Rousseauian, even though he'd abandoned his love of philosophy long before and now saw it as little more than a childhood disease that one had to suffer and recover from, the sooner the better. Which is why he didn't take the bait when I tried to respond to his probe with a diversionary tactic.

"But they're not superstitions," I said. "It's nature's way. Everything in nature has an effect on everything else, doesn't it? If the moon can move the tides, why shouldn't it be able to move something as inconsequential as a human being?"

"I knew that Leopold's gene for poetry had to have survived somewhere," he said and laughed. "Write that down so you don't forget it."

Suddenly I felt his mockery as though it were aimed at something that I meant seriously. Go on, I thought. Go to your study so I can think about this in peace.

"I'll go," he said, getting up suddenly, taking the napkin that had been in his lap and forcefully setting it on the table, where it soaked up a puddle of coffee.

"I'll see you this afternoon."

On his way out of the dining room he kissed me the way he'd kissed me on the way in, in his usual way that didn't require either thought or any emotional investment, like a clock whose hands can do nothing else but run their prescribed circuits indefinitely.

Other than that, he was right, I had slept badly.

I shouldn't have written to him. Wanda had always said that a woman can remain interesting to a man only if she gives him no sign that he means anything to her. If you can't project honest indifference, you're going to have to learn how to fake it. Nobody has ever yet fallen in love with a devoted girl. As a girl I was harsh to her in response. Maybe so, if you choose the wrong men, I chided her. If you'd found a man who really loved you, you wouldn't have to pretend. Miška, she'd reply, I'll be so happy for you if you find one. I really will, she'd say, stroking my hair. She loved me, but she doubted my certainty, and I didn't begin having doubts until several weeks after I'd met with Jakob at the Café Central, several days after I wrote him my second letter and waited in vain for an answer. Perhaps at last this was proof that Wanda was right. Or else I'd made a bad choice after all. In any case it would have been better if I hadn't written to him. If I'd waited for him to make the first move. But in order to wait, I would have had to know that it's a mistake for the woman to make the first move, but I really didn't know that, despite the number of times Wanda had warned me. When I chose Maximilian, he had already had his mind made up about me for so long that he did everything himself. When I wrote to Jakob the first time, he responded before I was even aware of what I had done. I had no other experience. So I'd lucked out, until I suddenly stopped lucking out and suddenly I was flooded with doubt. Had I guessed wrong? Did I perhaps not interest him at all? Had I made some mistake? Should I have been nicer to him, more understanding? Where had he vanished to, this man who just yesterday had seemed so present, so set on becoming part of my life? How had he just gone poof? Had something happened to him?

In response to his silence I felt the stirrings of a disquiet that I hadn't experienced for years, but which remained familiar to me none the less. It was the disquiet I had known as a child, but subsequently forgot, and although it had been in hiding for more than a decade, it returned unchanged and with all the force of some childhood emotion that we haven't since managed to sculpt into anything nobler. It was the disquiet that always attended Leopold's departures, which always announced themselves without any assurance of a return. They were like a punishment, his departures were, like a sign that we'd done something wrong and were going to have to pay for it with the loss of his grace. Leopold was not a violent man. He didn't scream or smash furniture, he didn't beat anyone and he only became verbally abusive when pushed to the extreme. His cruelty resorted to other means. When something wasn't going his way, he simply vanished. He ended the argument, took his coat off its hook and slammed the door shut behind him. Sometimes he'd come home the following morning. Sometimes not until the following week. As a result, things usually went his way. That's why, as I found out much later, Wanda would sometimes sleep with some man she found revolting, and then tell Leopold about it later, as though it were some caprice of her own choosing. That's why she sometimes wore fur coats when the temperature was almost a hundred degrees. That's why she sometimes cried in the pantry when she thought no one was listening. That's why, when she couldn't take any more and used some pretext to force Leopold to leave, she took all the blame on herself. She ought to be stronger, she often chided herself. If she were stronger, he wouldn't leave. And although I had learned early to understand she was wrong, I often felt the same thing. It was not Wanda but I who needed to be stronger. I needed to find a way of explaining to him all the reasons he couldn't leave. That Wanda hadn't meant any harm. That she loved him and would do anything to keep from losing him. Wanda was too wrapped up in it all and incapable of finding the right words, while I, who could look at everything from a distance, would have to find a way of explaining the situation to him so he really got it. If he really got it, he wouldn't disappear, or so I figured.

We would feel truly abject, Wanda and I, whenever Leopold vanished. Mitja and Sasha would be despondent, too, but their despondency turned out to be of the natural kind, the sorrow of children missing their father and thus angry at him, while ours bore some strange resemblance to guilt, sooty and black and full of admixtures that lent it weight until it became practically impossible to bear. He must be dead, I would think when he'd been absent for a number of days. We drove him away and now he's dead and we'll never have a chance to explain that it was all just a mistake.

Even now, with that disquiet returned, it returned with its distinctive opposite. Part of me wondered what I'd done wrong to cause Jakob to respond to my presence with silence, while another part of me was feverishly trying to guess if something fateful hadn't befallen him. Had a carriage run him over, drunk? Was he at home with pneumonia? Should I have chosen some more fetching clothing or used more refined words to come across as more interesting to him?

There was no antidote to this disquiet, nothing to completely fill the hole it had carved in my heart, the only thing that helped even a little bit was going out for a walk. It was as if the world suddenly began to spin with ever-increasing speed and the only way I could keep from being flung off its surface was to start walking at an ever-greater pace in the opposite direction. I had walked through the woods in Bruck. I had walked through Graz. Through the fields around Eczed. And now, after moving here almost a decade before and clinging to home like a sickly child, here I was walking through Vienna. I was able to watch the time that my walks took shorten. If at first it seemed that I needed just under an hour to get to the Prater, soon I could sense that my walk through the city took half as much time. I didn't walk to sight-see, and I didn't walk to be able to think, I walked to harmonize my body with my nervousness and thus notice it less, perhaps for the same reason, I thought, that's behind Jakob's knee constantly shaking. I would leave home after breakfast and return sometime in the evening, each time reinforced in my determination not to despair when I found out there was still no word from him.

Strangely, these long days of tramping around didn't cause me to bond with Vienna. Just the opposite: my neurosis lent this city, with which I'd never really made peace, an almost monstrous aspect. I did get to know it, the way a person only gets to know a city by losing himself in it, but the more I got to know it, the more revolting it seemed. It was that summer when the Viennese, one proverbial step behind the Parisians as always, discovered the cinema. There was a poster beckoning them into every other cellar with the promise of a show, but practically every one of them had a warning in bold print affixed to it that it was for gentlemen only. Everything that pretended to be entertainment in this city was designed to be off-putting, as if instructing you that, yes, there is beauty in the world, but it's not meant for you. Spring showers dampened the streets and shrouded the canopies with yellowish clouds, people rushed by in their mud-spattered raincoats, obviously intent on getting home as quickly as possible without incident. Spring, which had opened amid so much beauty, had suddenly become revolting, good only for tuberculosis and toads. But despite everything I had to keep walking. Wear out my shoes and my coat, trail long shadows that would disappear around corners, and then wonder if the man who had just gone down the stairs into some cellar with what had to be an under-aged prostitute might have been Jakob, or maybe just wore the same kind of hat.

I felt embarrassed by myself and I felt ashamed. If anybody paying close attention had asked me what was driving me through the streets of the city, I would have refused to reveal the cause of my anxiety at any cost. I often recalled Krafft-Ebing's disquisitions about how for every woman her love of the man she's chosen means everything: it's her purpose, it's all that feeds her will to live, it's all she's interested in and all she cares about, and how, because love plays such a decisive role in a woman's life, every woman is prepared to sacrifice anything for it, suffer anything, and risk anything, because without it, without love, her life is devoid of meaning. I remembered those words, because I know that I spent years mocking them, before they suddenly started dangerously resembling something that I felt myself. I became monomaniacal, but saw nothing exalted in that, just another cause for despair. It wasn't until I myself fell in love for the first time in my life that I realized how deep my resistance to love was. As if love were in some way related to humiliation, as if it made personal dignity impossible in some way.

As though I were trying to conceal the senselessness of my wanderings from some spy, perhaps even from myself, I began frequently stopping by Helene's house on my walks. Perhaps I had ulterior motives for doing that – perhaps I hoped that she, as securely ensconced in her social network as she was, might in one of her regular social registers reveal something about Jakob's disappearance – but if I did, I managed to conceal them even from myself.

Helene was happy to have tea with me and gave no hint of being aware that her company served me as an excuse. She liked to talk and had two favourite topics: interior decorating and the love life of Emilie Flöge. It was a pleasure to listen to her talk about household furnishings, even if, like me, you knew nothing about them. It was simply impossible to mock her devotion to material things, because there was nothing impure about that devotion. There was nothing she aspired to for the sake of boasting about it, or using it to compete with somebody. Rather, as I suspected then, she felt driven to immerse herself in beauty in order not to have to reconcile herself to death and decay, and there was something about that wish that moved me every time. It was somewhat less gratifying to listen to her talk about Emilie Flöge. Whenever Helene talked about Emilie, the cosmopolitanism in which she otherwise took so much justified pride would give way to a baffling pettiness.

"Klimt will never marry her," she was fond of declaring in a voice disguised as concern, as though their getting married meant more than anything in the world to her.

"She'll wait for him into old age, and she'll die childless and unhappy," she said, as though she believed that a woman's happiness was positively linked to children.

"Oh, I'm so sorry," she would say, as though she'd unintentionally offended me by saying that.

I shook my head. She hadn't offended me. "It's all right," I said.

I understood what she meant in my own way. Anyone who had encountered Klimt and Emilie could tell that there was something painfully out of balance about their relationship, something you could almost call unjust. And when Helene talked about them, it sounded as though what was at stake was personal, as though she needed Emilie so she could use her story as a foil to her own, thus underscoring her own success, her wise choices and rationality by contrast. As though she weren't condemning Klimt for mistreating her, but her for being in love with him in spite of everything. A woman in love inspires pity, Helene signaled through her statements, but pity is just another word for disdain. I would often leave her house with a heavier heart than when I arrived.

When I got back home at dusk, Maximilian was usually sitting at the dinner table, waiting for me. 'Did you have a nice time out in the fresh air?' he'd ask. Perhaps you'll sleep better tonight.

12 *I know it's not true*, Jakob wrote in his letter when it finally arrived, *but I still get a charge from thinking that you're related to old Sacher who baked the cakes for Metternich. I've thought about it so much that I've booked a room in their hotel. Have you ever been here? Do you know the owner? It's quite amusing to think how stubbornly that butcher's daughter and wife of a pimp has devoted herself to her ambition of ingratiating herself with Viennese high society and buying herself a place among them. Surely you see that. As though she's taken all that's worst about Austrian self-regard, made a bouquet of it, and set it out for all to see. I have the sense that they looked at me askance when I paid, but nobody ever says anything against money. And now I've had a cake brought up to the room. It's been years since I've eaten any desserts and I have to say it's a pleasant surprise. If only because in the whole wide world at last there's something that I have in common with Metternich. Deep down we're all bloodied, aren't we… If you get here quick, I can probably save you a piece.*

Was that an invitation? Should I have dropped everything, put on my overcoat and run towards the Sacher Hotel, or would I only humiliate myself in the process? I'm going out for a walk, I told myself, as though I were trying to conceal my real intention from myself. I'm just going out for a walk to think about some things.

"I'm going out for a walk," I told Maximilian, who was reading the newspaper in the salon.

"If we do decide to vacation in the Swiss Alps this year, I'd better not try to compete with you for speed, considering how much you've been training," he said without raising his head from his paper.

"Then it's best that we don't go anywhere," I said as if in jest, although the thought of leaving Vienna for any length of time was abhorrent to me.

Although my walks normally took me to the canal and across it, as though I were drawn to the water by some natural imperative, I wasn't really surprised when, barely five minutes out, before I'd had a chance to think anything over, I found myself standing outside the Sacher Hotel, which was in the opposite direction.

Best to get this over with as soon as possible, I thought, before I run into anybody. Mortified, I pushed the door open and, like a sinner forcing out a confession, said I'd come to visit Mr. Frischauer. Room 102, the clerk at the reception desk said without any interest. You're expected.

So it wasn't a trap or a mistake, I thought, but that thought didn't make me feel any better. What game is this I'm playing? something inside me said in a voice that I'd never heard before. Wasn't the whole point of Little Red Riding Hood to warn young girls not to go traipsing into some wolf's lair?

I stood outside the door to the room for a long time before knocking on it with a heavy hand.

He opened the door, dressed as though he'd just now come in off the street, too. Shoes tied, wearing his coat, he even still had his hat on his head. There was no evidence that he'd made himself at home, except that, on the table behind him, there really was a platter with a half-eaten cake.

"Have you come for dessert?" he asked in a serious tone that gave no hint whether he was really serious or if it was irony disguised as seriousness.

"I don't know what I've come for," I said in a sudden attack of sincerity. "I was hoping you'd be able to tell me."

"Have you had a look around?" he asked. "In the basement they still have a bordello, you know. Or rather, *les chambres séparées*, as it's called, so the high and mighty can go whoring without anyone sticking their nose in, except when expressly invited."

Suddenly I became aware of the almost didactic tone of his letter, and was afraid I'd miscalculated regarding the intent of our meeting.

"If your invitation was to show me the hypocrisy of Vienna's elite, you've wasted your money," I said. "Surely you know that I have an excellent view of it without having to go in the front door."

"To be perfectly honest," he said, suddenly sounding perfectly honest, "the only reason I invited you was so I could feast my eyes on you in peace."

The anxiety that had taken complete control of my life for the past month suddenly dissolved. As if I'd just entered a heated room from out of the cold, I felt a wave of warmth course through me.

"Would you like some cake?" he asked to end the silence. "It's not bad at all."

"No thanks, I'm not hungry," I said with feigned indifference, as if there were something dishonourable about admitting how much his attention meant to me and how happy he'd just made me.

"How about thirsty?" he asked, picking a bottle of champagne off the table.

"That, always," I said laughing and sat down on the sofa facing the table.

He filled two glasses and sat down beside me.

"Take your clothes off," he said.

Even back in the years when Maximilian and I still had sex, he would always approach me with the utmost shame, as though he were a bankrupt who had come to the bank to ask for a loan, and he kept his eyes fixed on the floor to avoid having to face his humiliation. He would turn off the lights and then turn around facing away from me while he took off his shirt and set it down on the floor with military punctiliousness. Farm maids and farm hands fucked, Maximilian must have thought, but you had to use all means available to protect a lady and above all your wife from the violence of physical love, if you could even use that word about it. It was as though he spent the rest of his life in penance for the day in Lindheim when he took advantage of my innocence, and I'd wager that he never even considered the possibility that it was his reserve that caused me such pain. If I had shown him that I actually wanted him, I believed then and to this day doubt I was wrong, he almost certainly would have hated me for it.

Wanda and Hulda had next to nothing in common, not desires nor expectations nor convictions, but they were both convinced that sexuality was something that a woman had to forgive a man for, to reduce the chances that he'd go look for it elsewhere, some place where her controlling hand couldn't reach, and because it was sadly the only way to make a woman a mother. Maybe the smartest thing for any woman to do, Wanda once said in a fit of rage, is to marry a homosexual.

Aside from Leopold, who everybody at least secretly suspected was insane, everyone around me was convinced that the body was something it would be best to dispel from their minds as completely as possible, and now here, in front of me, was sitting this man who was absolutely serious about his desire and seemed to expect an outpouring of lust from me. Suddenly I realized with perfect clarity that this was precisely what had drawn me to him in the first place. As I sat down on his lap naked, I became aware of my vulnerability with every part of my body, but that vulnerability, that nakedness through which you could see everything, was what

I had been longing for all along. It was as though decades of self-concealment fell away from me in an instant. As he lay with his face buried between my legs, intent on giving me pleasure, as though my pleasure were more important to him than his own, it struck me how easily the happiness I was experiencing now, almost by accident, could have bypassed me. If Wanda and Hulda had known what sex could be like, surely they would have thought differently about it. Leopold must have been a terrible lover, I thought.

Even though, aside from the pathetic sex I'd known with Maximilian, I'd had no other sexual experience, I sensed that Jakob knew what others didn't – he knew that sex was something that required the whole person, not something that could be limited to a utilitarian joining of genitalia, that you had to draw the entire human body into it, something that was fed by sight and touch equally, and with him it was as though parts of my body that I'd had no idea had any function suddenly acquired a meaning. When he lightly grazed his hand over my waist, I thought that a tenderness this intense had to mean love. To this day I haven't fully appreciated how wrong I was.

"You don't need to be careful," I said quietly when it seemed his restraint was nearing its limit. Even so, he was careful. There's been a misunderstanding, I thought. I couldn't have given him a child, but still it hurt to think he was taking such pains not to give me one. Was this something fleeting for him? Didn't he at least hope it would last?

As he lay next to me, seeming so fragile, the immense intimacy between us was suddenly replaced by a profound emptiness. His breathing was shallow amid his light sleep, as though he didn't have a care in the world, while I was trying to figure out how to get dressed in my clothes from the day before and how to put on my face from the day before so I could go back to my life from the day before as though nothing had changed. Part of me derided my emotional arousal, but despite the attempts of my reason to intervene, I could sense a dark flower expanding somewhere deep inside me, weighing my heart down with its thick, viscous weight.

"I'm going," I said.

Jakob lightly stirred from his sleep and kissed me on the shoulder.

"But you'll come back?" he said.

"Yes," I said, fully aware that I had no other choice.

"Did you have a good time?" he asked over my shoulder as he fastened my corset.

"Now you know the answer to that."

"I know nothing until you tell me."

How I wanted for him to mean by that that I should confide in him, explain everything to him, reveal my thoughts as I'd revealed my body, but something inside me commanded me to keep silent. That's just a manner of speaking, I thought. That's how you use words to create something that doesn't exist, that's how you entice someone to confide in you when there's not any material basis for them to do so. It made me afraid for myself. But still, as I left, I took one last look around. The room was saturated with disorder. Jakob was half sitting up in bed, tousled, propped up on his elbows. His hat had been hung over the empty bottle of champagne.

"Be careful walking home," he said laughing.

"All five minutes of the way, right?" I said with a broad grin, although what reigned inside me was gloom. I need a long walk, I thought. About the length of the Camino de Santiago. I gently shut the door behind me.

Maximilian was irritated when I got home, because we had a date with Helene and Wolfgang to go to hear Schönberg's "Transfigured Night", and I of course was making us late.

"It's nice that sporting activities mean so much to you, but nevertheless I wouldn't want to become known on account of you as a person who doesn't honour his obligations," he said.

What sporting activities? I felt confused and blushed slightly. Walking! Of course, walking.

"Give me a few minutes to fix myself up," I said as I turned away from him.

He scowled at me. "Hurry up!"

Being in a hurry did me good, because it kept me from thinking. I didn't get nervous again until Maximilian announced that he would like us to walk to the Musikverein.

"Now I'd like to have a nice walk," he said in a voice that allowed no argument.

Of course the route, though short, led past the Sacher Hotel. All the way I tried to look at the ground, as though worried that my shoes might get caught between paving stones. When I was almost sure that the worst was behind us, I heard a familiar voice call out from across the street.

"Moser," Jakob called out, already tipping his hat. Then, when he called out to me as "gnädige Frau," he even bowed slightly.

"Frischauer," Maximilian said, tipping the edge of his hat upward slightly. " I hope you won't be offended if there's no time to chat, but we're in a very great hurry."

"Oh, don't be ridiculous, I only wanted to say hello. Have a good evening."

He put the hat back on his tousled head and went on his way.

"It's funny, seeing a socialist like that leaving the Sacher Hotel. Dictatorship of the proletariat by all means, but luxury demands its due."

The rest of the way there I barely dared to breathe. What had come over Jakob for him to force that encounter? Did he like being a provocateur? Had I just been a cheap thrill for him?

The concert was a living nightmare. Squeezed in between Maximilian and Helene, who kept nodding their approval, the expressions on their faces signalling connoisseurship, I let the heavy music drop into me and feed my neurosis. I began to shred the programme like a child unable to sit still. Every so often Maximilian nudged me with his elbow to let me know how much I was bothering him. Get a grip on yourself, I thought. To make it at least look like I was paying attention, I forced myself to read the poem by Richard Dehmel that was printed on an insert in the programme. I've long since forgotten most of it, but the part that affected me so much at the time has stayed with me to this day. I walk beside you in sin, it went, I have committed mortal sin against you, abandoning all hope of happiness, yet longing for life… and then came the verses about motherhood, but at that point I couldn't read them, due to the thick, cool tears blurring my vision. I could no longer hope for happiness, and yet I still longed for life. I cried all the way till the applause. If anyone noticed, they certainly didn't mention it.

13 The way other ladies knitted, played the piano or discussed the woman question, I now had a lover. Regarding that, Freud had among other things a theory that I needed him to strengthen my position vis-à-vis Maximilian, to remind myself that I was the one who loved less, who had her own life on the side, the one who was less emotionally involved and thus less inclined to get weepy if something went wrong, the one who wasn't going to end up like Wanda. Despite the fact that this theory seemed logically impeccable, I never really believed it. I needed him because I needed love. Because I couldn't reconcile myself to the fact that somebody else's choice had shoved me into marriage, someone whom I most certainly would have despised, if the attention that he was prepared to lavish on me hadn't delivered him to me. I wanted to love the way men love women. So that I'd be the one to choose, I'd be the one attributing worth to the beloved, who might not even have any in his own right, I'd be the one to stare at his physical beauty as though he were an exhibit item, and credit it with metaphysical dimensions.

When Maximilian and I joined Helene and Wolfgang in Davos that summer, I expected that I would languish from missing Jakob, but I didn't. In fact it did me good, the distance and the time that went with it, time that I could use to think about him instead of being with him, to write to him and read his letters to me, to let words do the great work of creating intimacy without bodies having to be present.

Now that we're not together, he wrote, *I've once again set about reading Sacher-Masoch. I had almost forgotten what marvellous things he wrote. I even think now that what I recalled as being important about his work is actually only of secondary importance, that it was never so much a matter of his teaching me how not to be ashamed of my own race, but rather of teaching me how not to be ashamed of myself as a human being. That the things my own father, who was never able to reconcile himself to the fact that I was never going to take over his business, that I wasn't going to defend my honour with shouting and fisticuffs, that I couldn't and wouldn't become like him – that these things that my own father viewed as weakness and cowardice were perhaps things to which a person ought to aspire. That perhaps not we, but the people who saw violence and cruelty as manifestations of decisiveness were wrong. I know what you'll say. I know you'll reproach me for having overlooked critical passages in order to interpret him thus, but I want you to know that when I look at you I see in you traces of what your father has taught me. That you, with all your understanding, gentleness and humour, are a reflection of something that Sacher-Masoch understood, and though he perhaps didn't know how to carry it out in the most elegant way, at*

least he knew how to pass that knowledge on to others. I don't want
you to think that you have value for me just because you happen to be
his daughter. It's just gratifying for me to see how certain threads that
I didn't even realize passed through me come together in you. I hope,
though I know there's not much hope of it, that Switzerland isn't too
boring for you.

What sincere language this is, I thought, almost more so than the people who use it – how much truth there was in phrases like having value for someone or meaning something to someone, how clearly the phrasing signalled that there was nothing essential about love, that everything was relational. I didn't believe him when he wrote that I didn't have value for him just because I happened to be Leopold's daughter, but it didn't bother me, even if perhaps it should have. It was also endearing for me that this person, this almost-complete-stranger, should admire Leopold for all the same attributes that I did. Wouldn't Leopold have been fond of him, I thought, if he'd been able to know him. To think of all they could have talked about. Would Jakob have got him to talk about his father? To express his fear and insecurity, to break free of the tyrant against whom even death had been powerless? Jakob didn't know about these things, and as though I wanted to protect the image he had of Leopold, I never told him. Leopold knew how to be brave only when he was writing. Judging from the way he behaved around angry, power-obsessed people who carried some weight in the world, I seriously doubt that he ever defied his father. Leopold was intent on avoiding conflict at all cost, because, as he liked to say, he couldn't have endured it, and as a result he caused a lot of damage. And in some sense that really was cowardice.

As if my memory were trying to remind me of something, I suddenly recalled how wise and kind Leopold could sound when he invited his friends in Bruck to come play chess with him and discourse on human nature, how he would tell them that he only trusted women, because men in their cruelty were personally responsible for all of the ills of history, that women, if only by dint of the fact that they'd had to suffer so much at the hands of men, were always at least a little better and that the only thing a man could do, if he wanted to think of himself as a good person, was to become as much like women as possible, forsake all ambition to dominate and assume the role of the victim, turn the other cheek, and do penance for the historical guilt set on him at birth. And how he would force Wanda to sit with him and nod, how he would praise her to whichever interlocutor was present, "how strong my wife is," he'd say, "how kind and how beautiful, I can't think what I've done to earn her love, and yet she gives it. Isn't she perfect? Look at her, is it even possible not to fall in love with her? Haven't you perhaps also fallen in love with her, even just a little? It's all right, you can tell me frankly, I won't hold it against you, it's only natural for a person to be drawn to perfection. And you know," he said, "I came to the conclusion long ago that I can't keep such perfection just for myself, she deserves to be free and, what's worse, she has to be free. Go ahead, ask her if she'd like to give you a kiss, if you want her to, I certainly won't stand in the way. Who am I to prevent other people from being happy?"

I recall one of his friends, whose name I forgot long ago, once saying to Wanda, "I don't see how you can stand it. You do know that what he's doing with you verges on prostitution?"

Wanda just shrugged.

"He's complicated," she said. "But he's not a bad man."

"How can you say he isn't bad when he literally offers you to other men?" he asked.

"He's insecure," she said. "He worries that I might leave him, so he'd rather have some active role in it all than be powerless in the face of it."

"Even if that were true," the friend said, "it doesn't justify anything."

"Don't worry about me," she said. "It's not that important."

After that he stopped coming to visit, that particular friend.

I also remember how once, for my presumptive birthday, she showed me a letter he had written to her when he disappeared to Lemberg the year he discovered me.

Because it has recently become clear, he wrote, *that your love for me has reached a point where you'd prefer to see me hanging from the gallows, my determination that it is no longer possible for us to live together on the terms that you set yourself will probably come as a relief to you. I leave it to you to decide whether you would prefer to remain in Bruck or move elsewhere. If you choose the latter, I will of course remain here. If you prefer the former, I'll move away.*

"Do you know why he left?" she asked me.

I shook my head. I was seven years old. I knew nothing.

"Because a week after giving birth to Mitja I refused to sleep with some fellow he found for me through a want ad he'd placed in the *Wiener Tagblatt*."

Leopold knew what it meant to be a good person, but through his weakness he probably caused more damage than a person who openly declares himself an advocate of evil would.

As I compared the two, Jakob suddenly appeared to me as somebody who embodied all the things that were truly sterling about Leopold, as well as something else – that dash of arrogance that people needed in order to bridge their weaknesses. He was a person, I believed at the time, whom life had not driven to apathy, resentment and detachment, who had managed to withstand evil and injustice without becoming callous, and yet who was also capable of being decisive, without which any overt moral stance is nothing but platitudes. I so wished that he might be the person who was capable of being both gentle and brave at the same time, the person whom I had wanted to believe in, but whom life up to that point had persistently shown me almost certainly did not exist. I so wanted him to be like that, and he was only too happy to nurture my expectations – as, indeed, why wouldn't he be, considering how richly he was rewarded for that with affection and admiration?

During a climb up the Jakobshorn (the Jakobshorn! One more sign, as I thought to myself, that all of reality was confirming my love), as I listened to Maximilian describing to Wolfgang how lazy our servants were and how, considering the amount of energy it cost them to do the most elementary tasks, it was scarcely surprising that they had the jobs they did, because they'd be completely thwarted by any more challenging work, I thought about how he had become so wooden in recent years. I recalled Helene once characterizing him as stuffy, saying that he acted as though he had taken the place of their father, but I also recalled how different he'd been when I first met him, how I never would have been able to predict that he would grow into the kind of person who is capable of demonstrating their own reasonableness only through spite, who would be so anxious that people not see him as an indolent fool that he would have to constantly accuse others of indolence and stupidity. I looked at him, his face bulging and flushed as he huffed and puffed his way up the mountain, and I thought about how cruel people become when all they care about is appearing perfect to the world, and how much I loved Jakob for not being that way. At the time I truly was prepared to believe that his decision to take his imperfection as a given and build on that was in itself proof of character, as though sadness were in any way an ethical category.

For the longest time, I wrote to him, *I've wondered why I was so unhappy in Vienna all those years, but now I can see how little Vienna had to do with that. I was unhappy because the people surrounding me were so firmly convinced that people harden with age, that we have to become harsh and pitiless to protect ourselves from reality, that we have to renounce all vulnerability and, like a wolf among wolves, view everyone else with distrust. But now I know that it doesn't have to be that way. When I listen to you, I realize that the hope that I left behind me without ever noticing, withered away without any good reason.*

My readiness to fall in love with him perceived everything he said as solid proof of his greatness, of the fact that I didn't love him simply because I wanted to be in love, but because there was something about his human essence that was deserving of the kind of love that I felt, and because the world wasn't giving him the kind of recognition he deserved, it was only fitting that I teach him to love even more. When I arrived back in Vienna, I was absolutely certain that his objective decency fully justified my love.

We met at the Hotel Sacher, as though we'd been doing that all our lives, and we kissed as though we'd never in our lives kissed anyone else. What ensued was a long period of self-sufficient happiness. I won't say much about that – not because I don't think it makes sense to talk about happiness, but because any analysis would almost certainly reveal it as a figment of my imagination, and I long ago resolved to maintain certain lies as having been true, no matter what that might say about me.

14 For a long time I was convinced that my excursions to the Hotel Sacher had gone unnoticed. Or perhaps even worse: for a long time it didn't even occur to me that someone might be tailing me, and perhaps I wouldn't even have remembered this on my own, perhaps it would have remained too inconsequential forever, too concealed by the nagging wish to brag about my love, if one day a stout lady hadn't approached me in a cloud of cigar smoke, with a cloud of obnoxious French bulldogs yapping around her legs.

"Why don't you come have a cognac with me?" she said. It was Anna Sacher, the butcher's daughter and wife of a pimp, as Jakob had referred to her some years before. She was the hotel's owner. Her soft voice suggested she was inebriated. It was an invitation I couldn't refuse. Confide your secrets to me, it commanded, or else, instead of protecting them, I'll start spreading lies about you.

"I know most of the regular guests here," she said as we sat down in upholstered armchairs gracing her little Stammtisch. "So it's quite strange that you and I have never chatted. How long have you been coming here?"

I had to give it some thought at first. When I was finished, the number resounded inside me with uncanny certainty. Five years.

"Five years," I said.

Where on earth had five years gone? How had I managed to become someone who could be described as a regular guest of a particular hotel?

I became angry with her. Where did she get off grilling her guests with intimate questions? Weren't hoteliers supposed to be famous for their discretion?

"I don't mean you any harm," she said in response to the look on my face. "I just wanted to chat a bit. You know, woman to woman."

"So, you respect men too much to stick your nose into their business, but not women?"

Anna Sacher burst out laughing. "Let me repeat," she said. "I do not mean you any harm. Still, I would advise you to rein in that temper if you care at all about protecting your dirty conscience."

"Thanks for the advice," I said without any gratitude, abruptly got up and emptied the glass on the table in front of me in one gulp.

"No offense," her voice resonated drunkenly behind me as I walked away.

She had said nothing, Anna Sacher, nothing of any substance, nothing that might suggest that she secretly disapproved of me, nothing that I had any right to take offence at, and yet she had reminded me of something that throughout all those years gliding past I had been trying to forget. Over the years, Jakob had become my hobby, my afternoon amusement, my break from reality. Instead of my life with him replacing my life with Maximilian, it became its supplement. All I had to do was jot down the hours devoted to him in the schedule of my marital obligations and the business was done. Maximilian had the kind of wife he wanted, a wife who didn't complain and didn't needlessly extort conversations from him, while I had a welcome diversion that gave me the sense that my life was going somewhere and things were happening in it, without my having to give anything up. If our love had assumed the ongoing form of adultery, then, without any conventions or opportunism to hold it together, it was doomed to expire as soon as the thrill of its self-referentiality weakened, as soon as it lost its power to invalidate anything that led beyond its own bounds. But if it was meant to lead beyond itself, it was precisely at this moment mature enough to realize its fundamental contradiction. If we were as close as I liked to believe we were, why had we been living apart from each other for so long?

"You look worried," Jakob said as I came through the door into the hotel room. What an impossible space this room was, what a rift in time, what a fata morgana. How flabbily it clung to reality.

I shook my head. "I've just been thinking how much easier it must be to be a man."

Jakob smiled. "I suppose that could be arranged," he said and got up off the divan, heading towards the door.

Startled, I looked at him and shook my head once again. "Never mind, it's passed," I said, occupying the spot that he had occupied moments before.

"Oh come on, hold on just a minute, I'll be right back," he said and vanished out the door before I could even say that I wanted to talk.

I spent a long time drinking in silence. In fact, I didn't really want us to talk. And above all, I didn't want to have to explain anything. I wanted him to come to his own realization of the discordance of what we'd been living, so that perhaps he would start the discussion, would promise or give me something, and become the kind of man who predominated in penny novels, a man who takes the initiative, both saviour and saved. But it was just Jakob who returned about an hour later with an armful of boys' clothing, even a little cap, and said:

"Put these on and we'll go out."

Had he stolen them from his own son? Imported them from his real life?

"Come sit with me first," I said.

He sat, and although I tried determinedly to make my voice project seriousness, it didn't induce Jakob to wipe the idiotic boyish grin off his face.

"Tell me what's on your mind," he said.

Suddenly I felt as though my entire vocabulary had dried up.

"It's not important."

"Of course it's important."

"No, it isn't, forget it."

In order to avoid responsibility for the conversation I hoped for, but didn't want to have to initiate myself, I began changing into the clothes he'd brought me. The trousers were a little too short on me and the shoes were too big, but as soon as I put the cap on my head, I could swear I was a near-perfect copy of a young man with boyish features.

"You could seduce some homosexual without even trying," Jakob said, laughing. He was quite pleased with my costume.

I sat down beside him again. Perhaps it will be easier for me to talk to him if I actually pretend I'm not me any more, I told myself.

"Jakob, don't you find that there's something false about the way we've handled our love for each other?" I had to find roundabout ways of saying it, because too much directness would have exposed me too much. I could never have said, "Divorce her and live with me." I was much too afraid of the truth.

"Where are all these petit-bourgeois scruples coming from all of a sudden? Don't tell me you've gone Catholic?" He was visibly unprepared to discuss it. Suddenly I realized that Jakob, who had always become so talkative whenever there were serious issues to work through, particularly ones he would prefer to avoid, was every bit as loath to discuss things as Maximilian. At that instant even the tiny bit of courage I had left evaporated. I became suspicious and worried. What if only I saw what the two of us had as conflicted? Or even worse, what if I had wrongly assumed that what we had between us was love, and Jakob, like Maximilian, believed that there were certain women in the world whom you loved, and others whom you slept with, and the fact that he could sleep with me meant quite simply that he didn't love me?

I didn't say anything and just looked at him.

"Oh come on," he said, suddenly pressing me to himself. "Isn't what you and I have nice?"

I nodded. I didn't want to spoil the moment by poking around in murky waters. To be happy you have to be able to lie a bit, I suddenly realized.

"Shall we go out?" he asked.

"Let's go."

"Where to?"

"The cinema. So I can finally find out what gets shown there that they have to reserve movie nights for gentlemen only."

I really was curious, just as I was curious about everything else that Vienna withheld from me, everything else it denied me, everything it wanted to keep secret from or spare me. Besides, I figured you could probably keep quiet at the cinema without your silence reverberating too loudly.

At this Jakob laughed. "We can give it a try," he said, "but I have to tell you that to qualify as a gentleman not only do you have to be male, you have to be legal age, too, and with that cap I doubt anyone's going to believe you're a day over seventeen."

"Thanks for the compliment, but surely you've noticed the crow's feet around my eyes."

I'm old, I suddenly thought. I was thirty-three. By my age, Jesus Christ was already dead, a martyr for what he believed, while I hadn't been able to screw up enough courage to even start living.

"You're perfect," Jakob said and gave me a kiss on the cap. "But if you don't mind, I'm not going to hold your hand today, since that might give some people the wrong idea."

But you never hold my hand, I thought, though I said nothing. I have to dress up as a man for you to even be seen with me in public.

We walked there in silence and silently descended the stairs to a basement pub that on certain nights served as a cinema. The grinning doorman took Jakob's money and in exchange for a generous tip let his boy enter, too.

"The young must be educated," he said, exposing his gold teeth as though he were the living personification of a cliché.

In the corner of this dive there was a pianist who kept playing the most insipid waltzes at his piano. A series of French-made films was being projected onto a screen that covered almost the entire back wall. They were short and fast-moving, well suited to the upbeat mindlessness of the waltz, and although I knew that what I was looking at were images of real people, there was nothing human about them, nothing I could recognize, nothing that had any staying power and required reflection, everything appeared too quickly and then vanished as quickly and was far too desperate to come off as comedic for it to interest me. In one of the movies a maid who, dressed in a little black dress with a white apron, had just swept a floor, lay down on a bed and began pleasuring herself with the broom handle, only to be surprised less than a minute later by the master and mistress, who for the next half minute pretended to be outraged, but by the time a minute had passed were already naked and rolling around with her like two pigs in a sty. In less than three minutes the whole thing was over and greeted with brief applause, which was punctuated by whistles from various gentlemen in the auditorium who were trying their best to divide their attention between the film, their alcohol and each other, then followed by the next film, in which the lady of the house casts lustful looks through her bedroom window at the gardner, who with great dedication is tending her garden. Was the theme of the evening love between people of different social classes? I glanced at Jakob, a man who in this crowd of men was indistinguishable in every way from the others. If he was no better in any respect than anyone else, then why did I have to love him more than others? Couldn't I accept his ordinariness and forget him? And yet he was so handsome in the twilight, this man with the cheap taste in pornography.

Once the evening's motion-picture supply was exhausted, the man with the gold teeth announced that a special treat now awaited us, whereupon he brought a young gypsy woman dressed in a transparent harem costume out in front of the screen. Without any introduction she began dancing something that in all likelihood was supposed to resemble a belly dance. Although the gentlemen retained their jeering jollity, the genre suddenly veered from comedy to tragedy. Maybe it had to do with the proximity – between us and the girl, who by now was dancing among the tables with an almost childish lack of skill – since the cinematographic distance that would have smoothed out wrinkles and concealed the smell of stale sweat was gone, and this girl, who couldn't even have been of age yet, was completely here, with her forced seductiveness and poorly powdered bruises, and as sad as she seemed, sadder still was the way her sadness went unnoticed by everyone except me, the only person who for lack of desire couldn't disregard the fact that the person I was looking at was a real person, not just an apparition with no substance, the ghost of Salomé, suitable for household use. I looked at Jakob again. He seemed to be entirely untroubled.

Something has broken, I thought as he leaned me over the credenza that night and pulled off my trousers. Something in me had broken and who was to say if it could ever grow back together?

15 If anyone were to ask me how the affair ended, I would be tempted to feign common sense and say that I was the one who realized that there was no point in carrying on and called off what had been doomed from the very start to remain just an episode, but I would know I was lying.

When I refrained from writing to Jakob for a number of days, I didn't do it because I wanted to hide, but because I wanted to arouse some sense of guilt in him. Because I wanted him to know that he had hurt me in some way, so that he could try to figure out how on his own and then make amends. To a certain extent I succeeded.

I've offended you, he wrote, and *I'm sorry for that.* He was sorry, but he didn't know what it was he was supposed to be sorry about. *I shouldn't have taken you out amongst the barbarians and I ought to have sensed your discomfort, but I didn't. I took it all as good fun and noticed only far too late that you probably weren't enjoying yourself.*

And you were right, because in fact what goes on in those dives isn't good fun, every last compartment is filled with pain and poverty, and anyone who fails to notice that isn't a jot better than the high and mighty who line the pimps' pockets without giving a thought to the fact that they're trading in human lives. Let's go for a walk, if you want. Let's get away from human stupidity and just look at each other.

Just each other, I thought hopefully. Perhaps he does know how to go on after all, he just doesn't dare write it. But, as we walked alongside the canal, he gave no sign of knowing anything. It was as though he'd seized on my agreeing to meet as a sign of forgiveness and had decided that it would be smarter just to tell me how beautiful I was, that any more demanding subject would spoil the happiness that he'd barely managed to claw back, and that he had to use every available resource to keep reality from coming between us, as though it weren't already lying there, as cold and rigid as the body of a dead horse that out of politeness nobody mentions, even though everyone can smell the stench of it rotting. But he, Jakob, wasn't the only guilty party. I also tried to make sure to clear every destructive thought from my path, to focus on his hand as it reached for mine in the Prater, and allow myself to believe that love was more important than certainty and that, while I was looking away, somehow everything would work out behind my back.

In fact it was all of it so ludicrous, I longed so much to be allowed to do what men were allowed to do, to be able to love like a man, not to have to be ashamed of my desire, to have the right to find out what was going on behind closed doors where only men were allowed, and yet when it came to our love I suddenly wanted him to treat me like a woman. I resented Jakob for not doing anything, and yet neither did I do anything. If he really loved me, I had to believe, he'd fight for me, run off with me the way women are run off with, he'd come get me and not give me any choice and in the end I wouldn't have to be the one who abandoned Maximilian, the one who had to take responsibility for her choice, the one who had to feel guilty. I'd just be a woman who had no other choice. If he didn't do that, it meant he didn't really love me, and if he didn't love me, it would be mighty silly of me to sacrifice anything for him, now wouldn't it?

For a while everything went on as though nothing had changed. We met and made love, neither of us brought up anything tiresome, and we were careful to root anything that might have thwarted this routine out of our minds.

Then came the dream that revealed that you can't really forget something once you've become aware of it. In the dream I kept returning to the evening for gentlemen, except that this time the gentlemen were missing. The dive was empty, it was reminiscent of a dungeon, an antechamber of hell, it was even darker and more damp than it had been in reality, and the wall and ceiling moved in on you until they crushed you, the way a nutcracker squeezes and crushes a walnut. We were alone in the tavern – Jakob, the gypsy girl and I – except that I was tied to my chair, while the two of them made love in front of me as though they were alone in the world, as though no one were watching, least of all me, a woman of a certain age disguised as a teenaged boy, tied up with coarse rope.

How many more of them are there, I wondered the first time I awoke from that dream, sweating and agitated, how many women are there to whom Jakob makes love when he and I aren't together? The inchoate resentment I had felt towards him in recent weeks now finally showed its true face: I was jealous, but I didn't know how to handle jealousy. Although the people I'd grown up around had been jealous, they were also people who had forbidden themselves to be jealous with an almost fanatical intensity. A human being is not property, Leopold was fond of saying, even if he didn't believe it himself, each human being belongs to himself only and love that's not freely given is worthless. Even Wanda at least gave the appearance of agreeing with that interpretation. Every now and then she would settle his debts from whoring, and each time the firm hand of reality reminded her just who it was she was living with, the circles under her eyes became a bit more pronounced. But she never said anything. People are free, Leopold said, and whatever he said sounded true and fine. How can you fault a person who's free by nature for practising something that's arguably a manifestation of his very essence?

I felt guilty whenever I woke up feeling jealous. Who am I, an adulteress, to judge anyone else? Although not a believer, I was otherwise a good Christian. I didn't want to cast stones at others, burdened down as I was with my own sins. It was very important to me to shake off the expectations with which I had unwittingly and unintentionally burdened Jakob. I began to ardently wish for what we had together to be enough for me. To accept life as it presented itself. To quit snooping on other women and wondering – did you make love with him, too? Are you going to?

I gave it my best, and with time the dreams went away. But something far more agonizing took their place. One morning, when I woke up covered in pustules, I immediately knew with all available certainty that I had syphilis. I didn't want to talk about it with Wolfgang, not just because I didn't want to reveal my infidelity, but also because I felt I didn't need an expert opinion. I knew. I was dying. My brain was going to curdle the way Leopold's had, and I would die in the district asylum, abandoned and ridiculed, with a body that the disease would consume to a point beyond recognition, and a mind to match. Surely you know, Freud told me at one point, that you refused to seek medical attention not because you didn't need confirmation, but because you didn't want to be proven wrong. You wanted to believe you had syphilis, because that's how you could conceal from yourself what you wanted to keep concealed. I didn't know. Especially not at the time. I only felt a terror of death, of the destruction I'd brought on myself, of the inevitable catastrophe that, like syphilis, was just waiting to explode with full force.

When I met Jakob that day, I couldn't resist any longer. All the pretending had reached the breaking point.

"Something's wrong," he said when he kissed me at the door and my response was more distracted than he was accustomed to.

I'm going to have to force myself, I said to myself, and answer truthfully. Not just say, oh nothing, everything's fine, it will pass, let this cup pass from me, let this uncomfortable moment end and turn all by itself into something that's easier to live with.

"Jakob," I said as we sat down on the divan, "there's something serious that I need to ask you, but I don't know how."

He took note of my concern and responded to it. He leaned forward, as though he were trying to guarantee my safety with his body.

"Whatever it is, you can ask me."

Once again all words abandoned me.

"Have you ever been ill?" I asked vaguely.

He must have guessed what I was thinking, because he grinned ever so slightly when he replied:

"I've had recurrent pneumonia, why do you ask?"

I didn't want this to lurch into farce.

"You know what I mean. I woke up covered with spots and I'm worried that I've caught the French disease. Have you ever been ill? Please don't lie to me, I'll get through it somehow, but I have to get rid of this uncertainty if I'm ever going to get another moment's sleep."

He stopped grinning, took hold of both of my hands and looked me determinedly in the eye.

"I don't go whoring, Nada. I'm with you because I love you. I've never had syphilis."

He loves me, I thought, he said that he loves me. Was I out of danger? Was that the whole secret, all you had to do was say your fears out loud and they just melted in air?

"Would you leave Vienna with me?" I asked, emboldened by my unexpected success and halfway certain that with this admission of his love I had already been given assurance that I could continue with my demands. "Would you move to Lemberg with me?"

"I can't," he said in a dispassionate tone.

He didn't even have to think about it. He had known all along what his limits were. This was the truth I'd been determined to keep hidden from myself, the thing I avoided most, because I knew that it was going to change everything for me.

"I'm responsible for Rachael and the children," he added. "I couldn't live with myself if I abandoned them."

It was a noble reason, responsibility, and it sounded better than absence of love, and yet it was redeemable for nothing. If he was so concerned for their well-being, did he have no concern for mine?

"Well, what about me?" I asked. It wasn't the other women, the strangers on the street whom he'd never met, never made love to and never spoken to that I had to be jealous of – it was his family.

He was silent for a moment.

"If we part," he said, "we'll both grieve the loss. But if I leave them, they might not survive."

It was over. The war was irretrievably lost even before it began, his voice was telling me. There would be no bargaining. That was that. My enthusiasm imploded just as quickly as it had taken flight.

"And now?" I asked pathetically.

"Nothing," he said, shrugging. "Will I see you again?"

"I don't know. I have to think about it."

He nodded contritely. "I'll be waiting for you."

I took my time leaving, as though I were expecting him to keep me from going. Even as I closed the door behind me, I hoped that something might happen. It didn't.

16

A person can pretend for a long time. He can convince himself that his tooth doesn't really ache. He just ate something cold, he'll reassure himself. No need to worry, it will pass. Whenever one of Leopold's favourite cats got ill and began to visibly weaken, he would always spend a long time reassuring himself that it wasn't anything serious. She's just a little tired, he'd say. All she needs is a good rest and she'll be fine. I can still see myself, the way I understood with a child's clarity of vision that nothing was going to be fine, that there would be unavoidable pain, and how I wished that I as a five- or a seven- or a nine-year-old girl would be able to protect him from something from which there was no protection. Everything will be fine, I reassured him. Lies always sound more convincing when they're recited in chorus.

Anytime a person loves, the pretending becomes especially intense, particularly when he believes that his love represents fate or when he's stupidly convinced that fate means happiness. Look at the two of us, he thinks, has there ever been anything as meaningful between two people under the sun as there is between us? Have two people ever been so obviously suited to each other, has there ever been a love that was so meant to be? A person can even pretend when his love receives no confirmation, when the other doesn't perceive the absolute fit of their personalities with the same acuity, or the inevitability of their relationship, the fatefulness of their love, even when the other couldn't care less and is scarcely even aware that there's a person walking the earth, who tells anyone with the patience to listen how powerful the connection between them is. Even when the other tells him straight to his face, I don't love you, I don't care about you, you're in my way – even then a person can pretend. He hasn't seen the reality of it, the person reassures himself. He's been blinded, perhaps he's still mourning some loss, perhaps he's so fragile that he's reluctant to rush into a new love for fear it might crush him, perhaps he had a difficult childhood and finds it difficult to trust. But he'll see, sooner or later he has to see that you can't run away from a love like ours.

Once a person's spirit has found a suitable perch, once he's decided to trust something and opened the door to it, it's hard to convince him that he's made a mistake, invested badly, and that he needs to start the whole process over again somewhere else. There's just one emotion that's powerful enough to disrupt the force of habit, just one emotion that has a sobering effect so powerful that it's like dousing the person with cold water. That emotion is shame. And the longer the person has pretended, the more powerful it is.

As I left the Hotel Sacher that day, it was as though a veil had fallen from my eyes, as though I had only now truly gained perspective on my situation, only now fully realized how shameful it was in fact. I didn't feel deceived, so much as I felt stupid. Jakob hadn't lied to me, he'd given me no guarantees, had never mentioned anything that went beyond our immediate present – I had had to imagine all of that myself and then expect something that nobody in her right mind would ever have expected: to count on a future, about which even I had no clear idea what it was going to look like, except that it would be ours. But there was no us. There was just me, who at the age of thirty-three had indulged in a stupidity that a younger version of myself would have derided. I hope nobody knows about us, I thought as I closed myself away in my room, I hope nobody saw me putting myself to shame like that. Just the fact that I'd debased myself in front of Jakob was humiliating enough. The last thing I wanted was for there to have been witnesses.

It turned out that shame was a dynamic emotion that engages the whole person. Because, like the sun, it's impossible to look at it straight on, since it would burn the viewer's eyes out with its sheer force, shame demands of the person who is ashamed of something that he turn away from it with his utmost effort. Suddenly I began assiduously reading the daily press. I had an opinion about everything: it worried me that the conservatives had come to power in Germany, I was annoyed that a new psychiatric facility had been opened so far from town because I believed it was wrong to exclude the insane from human society. I helped Helene organize social events and saw to it that Jakob didn't get invited to them even by accident. When the first letter from him arrived, I allowed myself to make the tiniest slip: was he writing to say he was coming to get me? Had he reconsidered? No, he hadn't. He was worried about me and he missed me. But in all of his emotionality there still wasn't a trace of decisiveness. Shame didn't permit me to indulge my disappointment. Don't be an idiot, I warned myself. And I wasn't. I was highly rational, as rationality ran riot within me, growing like weeds, virtually matching the extent of Maximilian's. The next letter I didn't even open. I had to keep myself from engaging with his concern and his kindness, I had to forget that even he was capable of emotion. If I was going to forget, I had to forget he was a human being. I had to become ruthless.

And perhaps it would all have turned out as it had turned out for the thousands whom disillusionment had trained to adulthood, perhaps everything still could have turned out all right in its own dreary way, if only free will, true to its depiction in cheap novels, had belonged to just one of us, and the rest had had to accommodate it as best they could, if lives hadn't collided in the most inelegant possible way, if they hadn't run up against each other like sailboats in too small a marina, their masts causing a noise that was impossible to endure.

To this day I can't remember: was it the sixth of October 1907 when I ran into Maximilian at breakfast as he was leaning over his soft boiled egg as though someone had just died?

"Is anything wrong?" I asked.

Nearly half a year had passed since I'd last seen Jakob. His letters had long since stopped coming. I no longer expected him to appear out of nowhere, so I couldn't have guessed that he could have had anything to do with what was wrong.

"Jakob Frischauer has challenged me to a duel," Maximilian said in a voice that matched the look on his face.

Suddenly I felt feverish. He loves me, something buried deep down resounded inside me. This duel can't happen, resounded something from someplace else.

"What for?" I asked, as though it served my purpose to feign a lack of involvement.

"Because he's in love with you and he wants to free you from my chains, the way he wants to free the working class from the Habsburg yoke," he said in a tone of acid sarcasm.

"That's not what he wrote."

"How do you know?" he asked. "Were you sitting there when he wrote this?"

"Maximilian, surely you know that I didn't have anything to do with any of this."

"No, Nada, I don't know that. I don't know anything."

"But you're not going to go?"

"Of course I'll go," he said, as if he were responding to some particularly dim-witted question, as though there was something self-evident about going to fight a duel with somebody. "Of course I'm not going to let that person go around sullying your reputation and then call it love."

I didn't understand what was happening. Maximilian, who was always perfectly in control, had suddenly become a man determined to defend his wife's honour at all costs, as though that honour were something particularly valuable, as though honour were something a man couldn't live without, while I had no idea what it meant. It was an empty, stupid word that Maximilian used to substitute for something he felt but had no idea how to name. Whatever it was that was happening, it was beyond my control. I began to get nervous.

"I need to go to the office," Maximilian said as he got up and left the dining room without looking at me.

I hastily wrote to Jakob, but before I even had time to start wondering when he'd write back, he showed up at the front door

"Are you crazy?" I asked once I'd managed to smuggle him into my room and lock the door.

He smiled, as though I'd given him a particularly observant compliment.

"And what if Maximilian happened to be at home now?"

"I'll have to confront him sooner or later, won't I?" he said, still smiling.

"Stop that grinning. What kind of farce is this you're trying to orchestrate?"

"I had to get your attention somehow," he said in the same voice that Maximilian had used to talk about honour earlier that morning. I still didn't understand. Had I ever understood any man? Had I ever understood anyone?

"You couldn't commit to me while we were still seeing each other, and now you challenge my husband to a duel after a half-year's delay?" I became aware that I was yelling and lowered my voice. I was angry, and perhaps I'd been angry the whole time and just hadn't realized it. "A duel? How old are you, Jakob? And where is your famous responsibility now?"

"Is Moser going to accept?" he asked, as though he hadn't heard anything I'd just said to him.

"You knew perfectly well he'd accept. You had to know." Even though he didn't really know him, he had to know Maximilian far better than I ever had.

All of it was just so absurd. Duels were fought by drunken students and young soldiers determined to prove to themselves that they belonged to a class that had possibly never existed, and certainly doesn't today. Duels were a farce that I was convinced any sane person had to look down on, and yet all the signs were that two adult men, each of whom had a high estimation of his own intelligence, were fighting for my love, even though it was scarcely obvious that I had any left, and even if I did, it was highly unlikely I was going to grant it to the best swordsman or the fastest gun. How pleased Leopold would have been if he were still alive, I thought bitterly. This was a melodrama after his own heart.

Jakob took both of my hands and kissed me on the nose, as though that made everything good.

"Don't be upset, Nada," he said, as though I were the one who had done something irrational and had to be brought to account. "This is just a stupid formality. You know, of course, that it's been years since anybody was killed in a duel."

"Even if in the last fifty years only one person has died and that one person is one of you, it will have been one too many."

"Nobody is going to die," he said.

It's funny, I thought, how ready people are to guarantee things over which they have no control.

"Nobody is going to die," he repeated, as if embracing me with all of his body. "Nobody is going to die, and if you want us to move to Lemberg, we will. Would that still make you happy?"

I nodded slightly, without even knowing myself if I was serious. I wanted to believe him, but I didn't. Faith had never been my strong suit.

17 It was a torturous day, the day of the duel. For me it happened the way birth and death happen to a person – it was definitive, even if it wasn't an integral part of my life. Duels were a masculine business, and even though I was presumably the issue at stake, I wasn't permitted to be present. That should tell you a fair amount about how much love has to do with the women to whom it's addressed.

I rehearsed Jakob's arguments, the way children practise their multiplication tables. The more I repeated that it had been years since anyone had died in a duel, the more certain it seemed that nobody was going to die now. Nobody's going to die, Nada. Nobody's going to die. Barely had I begun to believe this, than Maximilian revealed that they were going to duel with pistols. In contrast to Jakob, I think Maximilian meant it the whole time. Perhaps he had to mean it, because he wasn't the one who had provoked the whole business, because he had been relegated to the inferior position with respect to the decision and that was something he couldn't endure. It wasn't my honour that was at stake, it was his.

Because I couldn't see Jakob in the days leading up to the duel, I focused my attention on him, Maximilian. Was he afraid? As he got dressed, did it occur to him that all these banal little tasks that made up a life might soon be brought to an end? As we had breakfast together, I glanced under the table at his knees. They weren't shaking the way Jakob's did. Was fear of death beneath his dignity?

Amidst this terror of uncertainty and misunderstanding my love was democratized. I was afraid for both of them and amidst my fear both of them gained in worth. They were both precious to me. I wasn't prepared to lose either of them. I wasn't prepared to accept responsibility for my own actions, which had led to something that I couldn't have foreseen.

"Are you sure this is absolutely necessary?" I asked Maximilian. He just nodded and disappeared into his rooms.

Are you sure this is absolutely necessary? I wrote to Jakob.

Don't worry, he wrote in reply.

I imagined him at home, where I had never been allowed to go, his leg shaking under the table. Did Rachael know? Was there some elegant way to let your wife know that you might die the next day for the sake of another woman?

Although to this day it strikes me as incredible, I slept through Maximilian's departure. I was nervous and all night I'd been pacing back and forth in my room, trying to relieve my headache with heroin. Shortly before dawn I had to lie down for a while. Just as long as I don't sleep through his departure, I told myself as my eyes closed. When Maximilian left at dawn, I was asleep.

Around noon Helene woke me up.

She was sitting on the edge of my bed like a ghost. Had she come to reproach me? Suddenly I realized I had no idea whether Maximilian had told her about the duel.

When I propped myself up on my elbows, she dropped onto me like a spruce being felled.

"What's happened?" I asked in a voice cracked by sleep.

"We don't know yet," she said, sobbing into my shoulder. "Nobody has said anything yet." She lay down beside me and fixed me with her weepy eyes. I had never before seen her sad, I remember thinking.

"I'm so sorry. For everything."

All she did was nod.

"Maximilian wrote to me yesterday," she said, "but I didn't open the letter until this morning."

"Do you blame me?"

"You know I don't."

"How should I know that?" I said in a weak attempt at humour.

"I'm just sorry you didn't tell me sooner."

She wanted to be my friend.

"I didn't think you'd understand."

"Oh, of course I would," she said.

She had wanted to be my friend, because she needed a friend herself.

"I know it sounds horrible, but I almost envy you."

I knew that a confession was coming, I just didn't know what of. She had been in love with Koloman Moser since she was sixteen years old, and that love of hers had persevered, as only a love that isn't too closely aligned with reality can. When she got married to Wolfgang to keep from angering her father, she was still in love with Koloman, and he loved her, too, she said, he must have loved her then and for a long time after, because for a long time she could count on him kissing her whenever she wanted, and being able to see him whenever she wanted, or speak to him whenever she wanted to tell him something, and for a long time it seemed that all her expectations would be fulfilled, and that she could live two lives at once without anybody reproaching her. But, like me, she was surprised to find out that people were capable of free will. The day came when Moser couldn't take it any longer. "I've tried to think you out of existence for so long that I've finally succeeded," he told her. He had pretended for so long, I thought, and then suddenly realized that he couldn't pretend any more.

Suddenly I understood everything, even Helene and her feigned perfection, her painstakingly sustained light-heartedness, her parties, the fury with which she latched on to the social circle to which the man she loved belonged, the anger she felt towards Emilie, which wasn't really anger, but envy, the envy she felt for a rival who had chosen love over security and thus opted for a whole different pack of misfortunes to the one she had chosen for herself. Poor Wolfgang, I thought, did he know that she had ordered her whole life around a man, and that man wasn't him?

It was strange, though not inappropriate, to find myself comforting someone when my own pain was so immediate. As I stroked her damp hair, her sadness comforted me at first. Pain is so democratic, I thought, that it doesn't just come for those who have built monuments to it and come to understand it as their second nature. It comes to everyone equally, like death, inevitably and for no reason. But the same thing that provided me some satisfaction for a moment turned into its opposite in no time at all.

I don't know a single woman who's happy, I suddenly thought. But had I known any happy men? Was happiness something that no human being could count on experiencing?

Helene and I were still lying on the bed when, late that evening, we heard the front door being unlocked. We glanced at each other. I now had at least half of the answer to my speculations. Hesitantly, we got up and went down the stairs to the main floor, like frightened girls expecting their parents to scold them for something they'd done wrong.

Maximilian was standing in the entryway, looking vanquished and stinking of alcohol.

"Go home," he said to Helene.

She looked at me as if she were waiting for my permission, at which I nodded, as though called on to grant it. She left.

"It's over," Maximilian said as he walked past me and up the stairs.

"What's over?" I asked, although the lump in my throat was telling me what was over.

Maximilian didn't respond, but continued to recede into the depths of the house.

"What's over?" I shouted after him, as though the force of my voice could shout down death and force it to retreat back where it had come from.

"What the blazes is over?"

I heard Maximilian lock the door to his bedroom upstairs.

I slumped down onto the floor beside the front door and began crying, although part of my mind was furiously trying to deal with the fact that Maximilian had given me no real response, which could well mean that Jakob was still alive. After all, he couldn't just die, could he? I mean, a person who was alive just a moment before, who had ideas and expectations like living people do, couldn't just be dead the next, a lifeless body that would never have another thought, could they?

All night long I cried by the front door and waited for some news to arrive, informing me that my worst fears were wrong and that it was right to hope, that it wasn't stupid of me to try to believe that everything could still be all right, that nothing terrible had happened, that I had simply misunderstood something. I completely forgot that I ought to have been feigning indifference.

Rachael's letter arrived with the first morning mail and put an end to my uncertainty. The tone of the writing wasn't agitated, but the handwriting undulated slightly in places where tears must have fallen on the paper.

Dear Madame, it began, *all night long I have been reading your letters, which I discovered in a drawer of my late husband's desk. Because it's evident from what you write that you consider yourself a sensitive individual and that you had the same high opinion of your lover, I would like to disabuse you of the illusion that there was anything at all exalted about your affair, and tell you that Jakob Frischauer left nothing but whoring debts and unpaid tavern tabs to his destitute family. In case you're tempted to view his death as an act of love, I will have to disappoint you. I lived with Jakob long enough to recognize his gesture as nothing more than his usual rash, imprudent thinking. As I imagine you, with your hair let down, dressed in your exquisitely chosen kimono, surrendering to your sorrow, I would just like you to know how fortunate you are to be able to indulge in the luxury of melancholy. Herewith I am also returning your letters, which I certainly have no intention of keeping. Regarding the scandal I fear that I'm unable to do anything. Sincerely, Rachael Frischauer.*

Perhaps she was right, although I suspect what really mattered most to her was wounding me, rather than serving the truth, but at this point I couldn't have cared less. In one fell swoop, death had erased all of Jakob's faults, everything he had ever done to hurt me, everything he had done wrong, and everything he hadn't done. In death he now stood before me, all charming and handsome, with all the attributes that had once made me so happy, but were now taken away from me forever.

With great effort I retreated to my rooms and locked the door. I had to make sure I wouldn't run into Maximilian. I wanted to devote all my attention to mourning, which I wasn't about to sully with the hatred I felt towards him.

Did men realize that the victor in any duel was the one who got killed? And if anybody tried to tell them that, would they even listen?

18 If I hadn't previously known what honour was about, mourning taught me all about it.

Don't look at me with those weepy eyes, I remember thinking the first few days following Jakob's death, when Helene still came to check in on me regularly. How else was I supposed to feel? I sensed that she pitied me and was using my sorrow as a benchmark to contrast with her own, so that hers could feel more acceptable and manageable by comparison, so that next to me, the madwoman, she might even feel normal. Perhaps none of what I felt was justified, but I didn't care. I was filled with my own pain and wanted to abandon myself to it, as though it were the last thing that still bound me to Jakob, and as if he were still living in some sense, as long as I mourned him. And yet I was still just vain enough that I didn't want anybody to catch me doing it.

Maximilian and I continued determinedly to avoid each other. I know that he was subpoenaed to appear in court on account of the duel, but, dutiful citizen from a good family that he was, he was also acquitted, which caused me to hate him even a bit more. I didn't want anything bad to happen to him, but I couldn't reconcile myself to the thought that a human life was worth so little. You could take it as though squashing a mosquito, and all that would happen to you was some minor inconvenience in court. I heard about all of this from the servants, just as they had to report to him every day that once again the missus had refused to eat anything. All that time they were stuck, our servants were, in the thankless position of having to guess at things and depend on their instincts, because neither of us was in any position to speak clearly and directly, irritable and disagreeable as we were. I didn't envy them, but I also didn't care enough to even try to behave any differently. I spent most of the time in my room, listening to operas on the Victrola. In the meantime, Jakob had been buried and I couldn't be there.

Nearly a month had passed when I was informed that Maximilian would like to speak with me. Just the thought of having to talk to him was agonizing, but I also realized that the situation as it then was, was unsustainable. Were we going to live out the rest of our lives in the same house, avoiding each other? Instinctively I expected that the only discussion we could have would be about how to separate with the least possible damage. But I was wrong.

We were sitting across from each other, as if composed in an official, artificial tableau designed to mimic a courtroom, when Maximilian calmly said that he had made some enquiries and found out that Steinhof had discreet, separate pavilions away from the main part of the hospital that could be rented, and where I could go to recover.

"So you want to commit me to an insane asylum," I said coldly.

It was understandable that he couldn't look me straight in the face. I couldn't bear looking at him, either. We were each feeling things that excluded and negated what the other was feeling, we reminded each other of misfortune and we had never, not even before, been able to find a language that could bridge the abyss between us. We were living proof that Wanda had been right when she bitterly claimed that there was nothing less natural in the world than marriage. It was natural that we wanted to get out of each other's way, but why couldn't we find a dignified way of doing that? And why was it so obvious to Maximilian that I was going to have to be the one to sacrifice her dignity in order to provide a break without necessitating divorce?

"Help you get better," he said. "Not commit you."

"In a psychiatric facility. Where they douse hysterical women with cold water to shock them back into their senses."

"Nada," he said and fell silent. It was the silence of a teacher who has grown sick of explaining the same material to his student for the hundredth time.

"What?"

"Surely you must see how much damage you're causing with this depression."

Because young women are forbidden very early on from giving too much rein to their anger, at first I had no way of gauging what was happening to me. What was happening in my ribcage and forcing its way up was completely physical, a caustic alert that what was happening to me had to be unjust. Maximilian and I never argued, each of us had been trained that any dignified person had to resist expressing their feelings too directly. He was too rational, while I was too convinced that, if I gave any evidence of the destructive forces inside me, I would be condemned to solitude, but suddenly solitude seemed like a blessing. It was certainly closer to the truth than whatever farce was playing itself out between us in the dining room.

"You're the one who shot and killed a person, not me," I said in a voice that barely pierced the ring that sorrow had tightened around my throat. This would be the perfect moment to lose my voice, I thought. But things never come when you ask for them.

"You know full well that that person shot himself, and I was just the accessory to his madness. If he'd sought help in time, we might all have avoided this unfortunate situation."

I was repulsed by the prospect that Maximilian, if left unchallenged, might end up playing the role of the only mentally balanced person trapped on a ship of fools.

"So, to sum up, I'm supposed to assume full responsibility for my own mental state, when you're the who went and shot a man dead, who, by the way, is responsible for that, too. Do you have any idea what you did? A man was walking around, breathing and speaking, his thoughts moved freely and came together in statements, he laughed and told jokes and now he'll never tell another joke again, ever, because you shot him!"

At my last use of the word shot I sobbed out loud.

"At least have enough respect," Maximilian said as if from the grave, "not to lament your lover in my presence."

That was the first time he indicated in any way whatever that he knew what had been at stake. I felt sorry for him, sorry that I'd hurt him, since I was still close enough to him that I could sense his own grief, as though it were also mine in some way, but the sober, forced rationalistic way he expressed it was abhorrent to me and only served to feed the hatred I was feeling towards him for being the person who had shot the man who, even though he wasn't my husband in the eyes of the law, was still enough a part of my body that, when he was killed, I felt one of my own limbs had been cut off. How horrific this has all turned out, I suddenly thought. But perhaps Maximilian was right. Perhaps I really was someone who caused pain wherever she went.

"I'm sorry," I suddenly said. And I really was sorry, sorry for everything.

"So am I," Maximilian replied.

It had been decades since we'd been this open with each other, if we'd ever been.

"I could try seeing Freud again."

"What for? Are you in such a hurry to find a new Jewish prick for yourself?"

I felt as though somebody had just taken an axe and hacked at my soul. It took my breath away. When it came to fighting, Maximilian's style was similar to Leopold's, I realized, in that he only showed understanding in order to make what followed hurt even more. I had no weapon to defend against that.

"I can't talk to you, Maximilian." I really didn't mean it as a reproach, it was simply the truth. I had no verbal response to his insult. It was impossible to express what I felt, which defied words.

"Too bad, because you're just going to have to."

How many times had he evaded conversations with me that I thought were necessary, even essential? Conversations that, if we'd had them at the time we should have, might have prevented the monstrous debt that we had to reckon with now.

"No, Maximilian. I don't have to do anything. Just to die."

I didn't mean to be dramatic. On the contrary, I'd meant to be slightly humourous, but my voice was so humourless that the words about death just remained suspended in air like the low cloud cover of late autumn.

I withdrew to my rooms and locked the door. Maximilian pounded on the door with his fists until he relented sometime towards evening.

The next morning I caught a train headed for Lemberg, alone. At that point I didn't know precisely what I was going to do, though I was half thinking I might try to realize a never-completed plan that Jakob and I had, while the other half of me felt compelled to visit the invisible roots that behind my back had formed me into a person condemned to unhappiness. Today, though, I think it was more a matter of wanting to force Maximilian into feeling remorse. Although I preferred to think I was leaving him, my resistance to him bound us tightly together. I was leaving him, though I was still caught up in us. It was precisely the way Leopold would have left.

I had also inherited from Leopold a predilection for third-class railway carriages. I had been shut away in my room for so long that the presence of strangers did me good, even if they were eating pickled beef and transporting live roosters in cages placed on the bench beside them. I was happy to be in motion, which provided a simulacrum of change. Perhaps now I'll finally be able to think things over in peace, I said to myself. I fell asleep almost before the train had left Vienna behind. Before I dropped off, I remember thinking how perspicacious Leopold had been when he said that human history only seemed to be the history of intellect, when in fact it was the history of passion.

19 My late mother used to say, the innkeeper said after listening to me uninterruptedly for nearly an hour, that working people don't have time to feel sorry for themselves.

It was part of a familiar refrain, what he said; but his tone of voice had changed in the meantime. I could even have sworn that I suddenly sensed some sympathy in it. As if, in my person, he were suddenly feeling sorry for all those people afflicted with luxury, people who never once in their life had to clean their own toilet, let alone somebody else's, and finally went insane from a surplus of leisure. As Leopold had, he must also have believed that there was such a thing as a natural human being, as yet unspoiled by modernity, who was so thoroughly caught up in the demands of survival from one day to the next that something as deformed as my life, for instance, could never have happened to him even by accident, except that, in contrast to Leopold, he would have taken great satisfaction in the fact that that natural human being was him. Like Helene's compassion, his also consisted in large part of a comparative analysis in which he came out looking like the more fortunate and, consequently, the better person, but I didn't begrudge him this. As I spoke, the bitterness had come dropping off of me like chunks of plaster. It felt good to talk. I was drunk and grateful to him for being willing to listen, even though my voice kept losing its clarity, and my thoughts their focus. As I sat there across from him, I began to welcome the thought that I might have just shared that brief précis of my life with my real father, but that neither of us would ever know if that was true. For a moment I was tempted to ask him if he was aware of having given any woman a child and never hearing anything more about it afterwards, but then I reconsidered. After all, it didn't really matter.

"So," I said, "you think I should buy a small farmstead somewhere near here and start digging it up with my own hands?"

"Oh, rubbish. You don't have anything to do with this place, roots or no roots. You're not going to want to hear this, but as far as I'm concerned, I think the cleverest thing would be for you to go back to your husband and play out the part that's been allotted to you. It's the people who resist their fate who wind up causing the most damage."

For an instant his own inconsistency flashed before my eyes. He was so committed to political change, and yet he believed it was wisest for a person to cling to his birthright as his one and only possible fate. He wasn't a bit more consistent than Leopold, whom he sneered at so readily. Was it impossible for a person to be in harmony with himself? How often had I opposed my own self without even noticing?

"I think it would be cleverest," I said, "if I go outside first and get some air. Thanks for listening to me."

"Oh!," he said, smiling. "It's what I do for a living."

On the way out I practically ran into two drunken Cossacks who came tumbling through the door as though they were alone in the world and crashed to a stop around the nearest table.

If I heard right, the shorter of the two ordered a bottle of vodka, incidentally calling the innkeeper a Jewish cunt in the process.

It was funny and sad at the same time to see how spontaneously that man, who had spent hours insisting to me that he belonged here, was suddenly being rejected. I could have hugged him if I didn't already have one foot out the door. Perhaps he and Leopold were wrong after all in insisting on the existence of a natural man.

Perhaps all of us were bound by equally loose ties to whatever represented fate to us.

As I wandered around Lemberg in the light snow, I realized how right the innkeeper had been. I had nothing in common with this place, it had nothing for me, there was no self-knowledge waiting for me to dig it out from under the snow and cobblestones. Leopold's mythomania aside, this was a foreign country for me, and yet that sense of foreignness felt comfortable. This was a transitional space where nobody knew anything about me, where nobody could fault me for anything, where nobody could ask me anything, and where nobody expected anything of me. It was a pocket sewn into the side of reality, where I could retreat to be alone with myself, as though there were nothing to bind me to people and human affairs.

Jakob's death gradually settled onto me as what it was: a hard fact against which I had no words. I knew the drill: I was going to have to forsake something that I had already taken to viewing as my future. I was going to have to learn to imagine a future beyond it. I already knew enough about grief to realize that actual loss wasn't the hardest part of it. The hardest part was forsaking the image of your own life that you'd begun confusing with life itself. I was incapable of doing any of that, but at least I could imagine a time when I might.

More out of curiosity than anything else I set out to find the forest where Leopold had presumably found me. By this point it came as no surprise that there was nothing hallowed about it. It was a forest like any other, in which the deciduous trees had already lost their leaves, and the ground was covered with a thin layer of snow. I thought about Leopold and instantly felt sorry for him. What could possibly have filled him with such a feeling of inadequacy that he was never able to accept anything in the form in which it offered itself? What could possibly have driven him to feel compelled to train his children to do likewise? Did everything have to be laden with symbolism in order to acquire any significance?

On the way back to my lodgings I paused for a moment outside the building where Leopold's father had served as chief of police, and suddenly I could see him so easily, Leopold as a child, Leopold not daring to say anything in his father's presence, Leopold watching bloodied, battered prisoners being dragged through the building as nightsticks continually poked at their ribs, Leopold being forced to watch the police breaking the arms and legs of Polish insurgents and not look away, so that he'd grow up into the kind of man that every respectable son of the empire needed to be.

To my surprise I became aware that suddenly I was able to remember him without that memory being a burden to me. Did that mean I could finally try to understand him? And if I succeeded, did that mean I could also learn to understand myself?

When Leopold longed for the lash, who was he trying to punish? Of course he was driven by guilt, but what was he guilty of? Was the Austrian in him thrashing the Ukrainian to drive the childlike barbarity out of him and fashion a man out of a raw, shapeless lump? Or was it the other way around, and the Ukrainian in him was beating the Austrian to punish him as he deserved for being the jailer of the prison of nations? And how often, if ever, had he realized that he was neither the one nor the other, just as nobody can ever be. Was that something he could understand only in theory? Did it seem to him in his weakness that the act of orchestrating his own degradation was the only way he could assert control? Or that it was only through punishment that he could get some respite from the ceaseless effort at control that mistrust engenders?

No, I still didn't understand him. And yet it seemed as though a heavy layer of clouds had been lifted from my understanding. Was that forgiveness?

I tried to get a glimpse of myself, as though observing myself through his eyes. I had not liberated the Slavs from enslavement to Austria and led them to a brighter tomorrow, and I had not gained command over human hearts. Outwardly the story of my life looked extremely banal, standing or falling in its banality with the men I had either loved too much or too little. I resembled very little of what he had predicted for me, but what I did resemble quite a bit was him. I conformed with what he had taught me by his actions far more than with what he taught me with words. I was a faithful likeness of all of his contradictions. Like him, wherever I settled down I generated chaos, and then consistently forgot to take responsibility for it. Would he have been disappointed? Would it all have been vaguely distasteful to him?

It turned out that I didn't understand myself now any better than before, either, except that now I suddenly began to feel, bearing down on myself, the weight with which I had formerly burdened my recollections of Leopold. If I was good at condemning him, if I readily ascribed responsibility to him for everything he had or hadn't done, then I needed to be ready to condemn myself, too. If I could fault him for never managing to see the needs of others amidst all his concern for himself, was that perhaps the moment for me finally to do what he never could: discount myself and try to understand what I needed to do in order to be in others' way as little as possible?

Had the innkeeper also been right about my needing to go back to Maximilian and embrace the fate that I had pledged myself to on the day we were married? Accept Vienna as my home and make peace with it, instead of constantly looking over my shoulder in search of something more suitable? Reconcile myself to things as they were? There was no guarantee that, if I did go back, Maximilian was going to take me back in, but suddenly it seemed important to try.

When I got back to the inn, there was nothing but evidence of mayhem in the taproom. The tables had been overturned, the chairs were broken, and the innkeeper, his head scratched and contused, was haphazardly sweeping up shards of glass.

"Have you been robbed?" I worriedly asked.

"Only of my dignity," he answered peevishly.

"Can I put a bandage on that?" There was a mean-looking wound on his forehead.

"The biggest favour you can do me will be to turn around and go to bed immediately." He obviously put great stock in preserving his dignity.

"But what if I promise to just bandage the wound and not pity you while I'm doing it?" I asked.

"Is that even possible?" he asked in all seriousness.

"I hope so. Come on, have a seat."

And he sat down.

"Do you have any bandages anywhere?"

"There ought to be something under the bar."

I rummaged through the bar cabinets, found a clean rag and bandage, took a bottle of vodka off the shelf behind the bar and got to work. He didn't make a peep as I disinfected the wound.

"Let's say we're even now," he said when I finished.

"Because we've seen each other in all our misery?"

"We just won't tell anyone about that, all right?" he asked, as though we had mutual friends whom I might embarrass him in front of. But it was a nice pledge and I agreed to it. I still liked to think of him as my father, although perhaps he wasn't really. He and Leopold would have complemented each other so.

"Not a soul," I said as we shook hands.

"Now you really do need to go to sleep. I can't clean up here with you underfoot."

So I went. As I was leaving the inn the next morning I didn't run into him again. I settled my bill with the stocky lady who may have been his wife. She was also blessed with a kind of innate peevishness.

The whole way home I tried to guess what I might be walking into when I got back to Vienna, but it was almost better not to think about it. When I came in the front door I re-entered the same scene I had left behind just days before, except that Maximilian seemed to be slightly more tired this time and had evidently been drinking a lot while I was away.

He was sitting at the dining-room table, as though he'd been waiting for me to come back the whole time, as though he knew I would come back, as though I didn't really have any choice.

We were sitting across from each other again, only now there was no more anger or hatred between us. We were both too exhausted to entertain powerful feelings.

"Are you going to stay?" he asked.

"Do you want me to?"

"Would you get medical help?"

"Could I see Freud?"

In the gaps between the questions each of us nodded faintly. Because we were both prepared to agree to anything, our peace negotiations reached a speedy conclusion.

"I'm going upstairs, the trip was exhausting."

Maximilian just nodded. He didn't ask where I'd been.

As I was still trying to get to sleep late that same night, I could hear someone knock on my door, push it slightly open before I'd had a chance to reply, walk across the room, lie down beside me and put his arm around my waist.

I could tell from the hesitation in his movements that he'd had to summon a great deal of courage just to come in, and I wanted him to feel welcome, I wanted to protect him from being disappointed, the way I'd once refrained from telling Leopold that he'd cited some historical event. I put my hand on his, but the warmth of my gesture was feigned warmth. There was still so much empty space between us. Although both of us practised deep breathing with our eyes closed, I don't think either one of us slept that night at all.

20 "You probably know," Freud said as he glanced towards the cigarette case that I kept opening and closing instead of saying anything about myself, "that every box metaphorically represents female genitalia?"

For quite some time I'd had mixed feelings about the vulgarity that he paraded as clinical expertise. I almost felt flattered that he made no effort to protect me from it, as though he were doing me some special honour by that, as if it meant he saw me as an equal, that he respected me, that he knew I could take what he himself was able to take, yet in his own way he was also insulting me with his brutal reductionist thought, which kept trying to impress on me that I was never going to be able to understand the motives for my actions until I learned to see them in all their banality. The truth is ugly, was the subtext of everything he said, and if at times it doesn't appear to be ugly, then that's almost certainly the telltale sign of a lie.

"I absolutely know," I told him, "that you think that every box metaphorically represents female genitalia."

"Are you trying to seduce me?" he said almost mischievously.

"Would you like me to?"

"Let me phrase that differently – who am I a substitute for, in your eyes, that you deem it worthwhile to seduce me?"

A Jewish prick, memory prompted.

Not just Maximilian, but Freud, too, had become convinced that in my eyes he had come to serve as a substitute for Jakob, and in that sense each of them was right in his own way, although at that point neither one of them would ever have been able to admit it. Freud had become situated in Vienna by dint of the same forces that had been operative for Jakob, and it was so easy to bait him into an argument with me about the Jewish state, because those were things that he himself was able to remain professional about only with the greatest difficulty, even though he always went to great efforts to stop me as soon as possible. Jakob was still very much alive in my heart. I had loved him for so long that whatever had been his was now also mine, to the extent that I even talked like him with respect both to word choice and meanings, and I even felt things the way I thought he had felt, to the extent that I had even become a Jewish socialist who had renounced her tribe in the name of the International, and although I didn't say that to Freud, he knew. Even though his hunches were frequently wrong, sometimes he guessed right, and as a person who tried hard to conceal certain things even from myself, I found that hard to take.

"Don't you believe that a woman might want to seduce you for your own sake?"

"It seems to be important to you that we talk about me instead of you," he said.

That was true, too. For somebody who had been waiting her whole life for somebody to focus on her and ask her what she was feeling, I responded to Freud's expectation that I talk about myself with remarkable resistance, driven mainly by shame. It wasn't that I didn't know what to talk about, or that I felt I didn't understand myself. I had – or at least thought that I had – a complete overview of my life and emotions, except that nearly everything about it struck me as idiotic and shameful and I couldn't reconcile myself to explaining this to anyone. I wanted to talk about things that at least had the appearance of being external to me, things that would show me to be what I wanted to be: insightful, detached and rational. Suddenly it turned out that my vanity, which for the longest time I didn't even know that I had, had expanded beyond all bounds and commandeered my mentality. The more vulnerable I was, the less I wanted anyone to know about that.

I went to see Freud as though I were going to work. Four times a week I would lie back on his analyst's couch next to a wall whose every square inch was covered with pictures, and I would try to prime myself to say something truthful about myself, even though it seemed as though Freud was also perfectly happy with lies, because they posed a particular challenge for him. I would arrive and talk and talk and talk for three magnificent hours, which Maximilian gladly paid for, and all of us felt as though we were doing something meaningful, even though each of us was simply confirming whatever nonsense he was most attached to.

I would also come home as though I were going to work. There had been something reminiscent of penitence in the way I had decided to go back to Maximilian. We tried to sleep together again, although neither of us was much given to the idea. We had breakfast together and attended social events where we cast each other counterfeit looks of affection. We had never before given such a harmonious impression. How happy they must be together, people must have been saying.

Sometimes, in the evenings, I could sense that this farce had burst, like a bear stomping on thin ice. As much as I tried to keep my thoughts under control, every now and then a stray one would creep in over which I had no control. How am I supposed to live with this person when I had wanted so much for another to love me? I would hear one of them resound in the dark before sinking back into it. How am I supposed to prove to myself that there's anything real about this?

On the anniversary of Jakob's death my self-deception suddenly gave way to a flood of genuine sorrow. All at once I felt so guilty and I went to my appointments with Freud as though to confession. Was I so heartless that I had completely forgotten my love for that kind man who shouldn't have had to die, if only I had been capable of behaving more reasonably? One day I arrived and, as I myself believed, for the first time in the course of the ten months that I'd been a regular visitor to the analyst's couch at number 19 Berggasse, said something truthful. The truth, as I thought at the time, was that something beautiful hadn't been able come to life, because reality was arranged in such a way that it murdered all beautiful things before they managed to come to fruition, while I was guilty of not doing anything to prevent it.

To my surprise Freud didn't react differently in any noticeable way to what I experienced as the truth of my situation than he did to things I openly lied about. I was just about ready to hate him, this person who assumed the voice of God and rejected the things I believed in. I had loved Jakob, and loved him because he was a good person. Any evidence to the contrary threatened me. Freud threatened me.

"Your resistance is very strong," he said.

"What about yours?" I asked. "How strong must your resistance be that you can't even give me the most basic acknowledgement that I'm telling the truth?"

"You had to believe that Jakob Frischauer was not a bad person in order to be able to fall in love with him, and you had to fall in love with him in order for your life to become what it became," he said at my next appointment, thereby depriving me in the name of science of any possibility of believing there was anything pure about love. Instead, everything amounted to a fastidious keeping of accounts that took place somewhere deep down inside us, without our even being aware of it.

Freud thought that I had needed to have Jakob in my life for several reasons, not all of which were particularly compatible with the others. Given that he didn't believe the human mind was consistent, he didn't lose much sleep over that.

"You had to come up with him," he said, "because you needed to establish a better negotiating position with respect to your husband. You had to be the one cheating, you had to be the one who had the option of leaving at any moment, the one who had the buffer of not being trapped, just as you'd learned from the example of your mother, who had never been capable of such detachment, as she told you, and your father, who had a gift for it, as he showed you."

"You had to come up with him," he said on another occasion, "because you needed someone to rescue you from a relationship that you could never have left on your own, someone to play the role of the gypsy bandit who, in the dead of night, abducts you against your will from the confines of your life, offering you the chance for a new life, someone who could handle the hardship of divorce on your behalf, who could represent the hand of fate, which you yourself were powerless against."

"You had to come up with him," he said finally, "because he made it possible for you to live the way you'd been raised, a life driven by confusion and chaos, a life in which things only happen when they're driven by something destructive, and love is meaningful only when it's constantly under some sort of threat. He made the kind of life possible for you that you'd only known at home growing up, that you were used to, and that you had to repeat, because you found the promise of unmitigated happiness, the likes of which you'd never encountered before, too threatening, because it was too new for you and you didn't know where to put it."

What Freud's devaluation of my love for Jakob left me with was almost as painful as Jakob's death, because it brought home to me that everything I had felt for him was unfounded, without any material basis. That I had in essence invented the vulnerable, poorly situated man whom I felt so much compassion for and, in my own way, had even exalted, while in all likelihood the real Jakob Frischauer was just a third-rate skirt-chaser who liked to make a big show of his socialism and his pity, while in fact he sowed nothing but grief, misery and division wherever he went. Anxiously, I recalled the letter that Rachael had sent me when he died. *In case you're tempted to view his death as an act of love, I will have to disappoint you.* Now Freud was urging me to take on the same disappointment, but I couldn't accept it. If I did, I would have had to leave the memory of Jakob behind and try to move on. But that, as Freud well knew, was something I didn't want to do. There was no consolation in moving on, if everything that lay before you was empty.

And yet nothing Freud told me could have affected me the way it did if I didn't believe it was true. If it hadn't been for the nagging memory of how much I'd wished for Jakob to make a different future possible for me, and of how dismissively he rejected that wish; if I hadn't sensed that I'd had to invest all of my trust in someone who would treat it irresponsibly; if I hadn't for quite a while already suspected that nobody, including myself, had ever acted out of pure motives; if I hadn't been aware for some time already of man's inherent selfishness; if I hadn't for some time been certain that life didn't amount to more than a ceaseless struggle of all against all. The problem was just that, for me, in love I hoped more than anything else that life itself would prove to me how wrong I was. And reconciling myself to the fact that it hadn't, in fact meant reconciling myself to the fact that it had no intention of doing that in the future, either.

"You're sad," Maximilian said as we sat at dinner on one of those evenings.

He was right. The more I devoted myself to my grief, the more endless it seemed and I almost began to believe that nothing else existed beyond it.

I nodded.

"Just thinking out loud," he said as a way of signalling to me to judge for myself whether I was going to take what he was about to tell me seriously, "but does it really make sense for you to see Freud if it just makes you even more unhappy?"

I know that Maximilian didn't suggest that out of concern for me. He suggested it out of fear of my sorrow, which he still blamed for everything grim that took place between us, but this time his concern struck a chord for me. If dredging through the truth resulted in so much pain for people, didn't that perhaps mean that truth was something it would be best just to leave alone? Perhaps not all of us were strong enough to delve deep down into our own darkness and emerge from it unscathed.

"Do you think," I asked him, hoping he would make the decision for me, "that I should stop going?"

"See what you think," he said. "But it's hard to see you this way."

Although our marriage had for years already consisted almost exclusively of suppressed half-truths and even fully fledged lies, I suddenly felt bound to him by a deep sense of partnership, and it didn't even occur to me that that this unexpected intimacy between us was merely the result of his having just affirmed something that I had long since come to see as untrue, but still wished that it weren't.

I nodded again.

"I'll give it some thought."

When I told Freud that I wouldn't be coming for any more sessions, he looked at me like a man whom the girls had rejected ever since he was an adolescent, as though he were looking at his last chance at a fiancée, who had come to tell him that she couldn't really love him, however much she may have wished that she could.

"Do you realize how many people withdraw from analysis just when they're on the verge of a breakthrough?" he said in a voice that was outwardly calm, but bore the seeds of disappointment and anger. "How many people run away, just before they might otherwise have discovered what has been haunting them all along?"

"Doesn't that suggest to you that people might not want to discover it?"

"Mrs. Moser," he said, and the disappointment in his voice grew from an undertone to its dominant melody, "surely you know that people want all kinds of things that do them no good."

Suddenly I couldn't bear his patronizing tone any more.

"You know, to tell you the truth, I couldn't say if our sessions serve any other purpose than keeping your wallet full."

He said nothing and just looked at me. When I got up off the couch and bade him farewell at the door, he was still silent.

21 Up until that summer, when a letter arrived from Ruslana in which she wrote that she could no longer provide single-handedly for her and Maximilian's child, I remained quietly convinced that I alone was at fault for everything that had gone wrong with my life. Even though I was ready to swear in the same breath that an individual had hardly any control over his own fate and that, in a world ruled by death, there was hardly any difference between crawling into bed to await its arrival and striving for a life of action in spite of it, I continued to trust to my sense, which I must have inherited from Leopold, that there was something wrong with me, and so it shouldn't be any surprise that everything I touched collapsed catastrophically.

And because I believed that I created my own unhappiness, in the years after Jakob's death I also learned to believe that I could best manage to avoid it by forsaking any desire to engage with the world, by being active within it, or by inhabiting it as though it were naturally mine. That's why, on the day when Maximilian once again summoned me to a meeting in the dining room, I broke out in a cold sweat. What on earth could have gone wrong, considering I hadn't done anything? Ever since I'd stopped seeing Freud, I spent most of my time in the living room reading sentimental novels in order to avoid having to think about my own life. It wasn't as though I had any old secrets that could suddenly spring to light. It didn't even occur to me that it could be something that had happened beyond the trajectory of my own fault.

"What's wrong?" I asked before I'd even properly sat down.

"Please sit," Maximilian said. I was already worried, but his officious tone practically drove me out of my mind.

"What is happening, Maximilian?"

He was holding a letter, which he kept nervously folding and unfolding.

"It's from Ruslana."

Did we know a Ruslana? I had completely forgotten about her, my maid from Kolomiya, whom I'd forced to sing so I could wallow in my sorrow more easily, the maid who years before had imperceptibly disappeared from my service.

"What does she say?" I asked once I'd recalled her to mind.

"She's asking me to send her a monthly allowance so she can cover the costs of raising her daughter," he said, as if reading from a ledger of accounts.

"And just why should you be paying for her daughter?" I said, although a feeling in my stomach was already telling me what we were talking about.

"Because she's mine." He gave no sign of feeling even the least bit awkward.

"How old is the child?"

"Thirteen," he said. "Almost grown up."

So you wanted to send me to an insane asylum pretty much just for falling in love, while you were off fucking my chambermaid instead of staying beside me while I grieved for the loss of our child? What stopped me next wasn't good manners, it was the sheer weight of the revelation. Even before I opened my mouth, I realized I couldn't say anything. My shoulders grew heavy and everything inside me slowed down to the level of sleep. It was as though I had died, even though I still lived. Now I'd gone mute again. Why was it always letters that caused my aphonia?

"If you agree," Maximilian said, still impeccable in his formality, "I'll authorize a modest allowance for her so that we can avoid any further unpleasantness. We have enough savings to be able to afford as much, without incurring too much of a loss."

So you've just now found out, I wanted to say as I silently began cursing the fact that I couldn't produce even the tiniest squeak, that you have a daughter, that some thirteen-year-old girl has grown up without you and some woman with the barest of means has managed to care for her without any involvement from you, and you call that an unpleasantness that needs to be dealt with, to be got rid of as soon as possible? Maximilian, are you even human any more? It wasn't so much that I felt sympathy for Ruslana and her daughter, as that everything in me had suddenly come to hate Maximilian.

A number of things that I'd been avoiding practically my entire adult life suddenly surfaced, demanding my attention. The most insistent of them was Anna's death.

I recalled how I had once written to Jakob that I'd been unhappy my first ten years in Vienna, because I was disappointed with people and their rudeness, as though anyone had ever been made unhappy by something as abstract as human nature broadly conceived, as though it wasn't always concrete things aimed directly at us as individuals that actually hurt. In fact, I'd been unhappy on account of entirely practical, entirely personal things, I'd been unhappy over losing a child, and if I'd been disillusioned, it wasn't with people in general, but with Maximilian, who dealt with grief even worse than I did. But that would have sounded so petty and so mundane that I could never really have admitted it, even to myself.

In 1897 Wolfgang had confirmed my suspicion that I was expecting a baby. And I really was expecting it – expecting it in a way that almost prevented me from ever becoming a good mother, because I was expecting it as though, by saving that child, I was also going to save myself. If I had ever told Freud about that, he would probably have told me that Leopold had raised me to think that way, even though it hadn't served me particularly well. It's going to be a girl, I was sure, she'll have red hair like me, but a more delicate face, she'll run around the forest with just as much curiosity and play the piano, she'll love to read and I'll do everything to support that, she can marry late, if she wants, even though she's bound to be adored and loved by everyone, clever and sweet, smart and refined as she'll be. I'll name her Anna. Even though she'll be sensitive like me, she'll be at home in the world every bit as much as Maximilian.

Maximilian seemed to be happy, too. After three years together we had finally reached the last milestone that separated us from having everything. He reviewed his expectations and ascertained with evident satisfaction that he was becoming the person he had always wanted to be. Nobody could reproach him for anything, people could look on him with admiration and envy, and his difficult wife suddenly appeared to have become less so. And he still had a full head of hair.

Perhaps because I'd had so few real responsibilities in my life, the thought of parenthood filled me with the sense that, with the child, my life would finally acquire some meaning. I'm not going to be the kind of mother Wanda was, I thought, and I'm not going to be the kind Hulda was, either. I'm not going to hand my child over to the servants, I'm going to be with her, I'll be responsible for her upbringing, I'll talk to her as though she's a person, not some little creature who happens to live in our house. I wanted so much to prove myself as a mother that I tried as completely as possible to suppress all of the fears that my changing body had filled me with. If only I hadn't been so persistent about that, I might have noticed sooner that something was wrong. But I didn't. Whenever anyone asked me how I felt, I would always insist I felt great. No, the blood and the pain, they don't frighten me, I'm not afraid of dying, I don't think of childbirth as something frightening, like dismemberment, an antechamber of death, I don't think about it at all, not a thing, and I feel great and I can hardly wait to become a mother. Will it be soon? I'd wonder each morning. Let it be soon, let it be over with, let's get on with whatever comes afterward.

Ultimately, it came too soon. I gave birth to a little girl, but she was too tiny and fragile to survive without me, and as I lay half-conscious in bed, soaked in my own blood, I could hear Wolfgang saying to Maximilian that we should be grateful that at least I had survived. When he spoke to me a few days later, he cautiously told me that it was almost certain I would never be able to get pregnant again.

At first Maximilian was angry with me. Not because I hadn't and now never would give him an heir, but rather because he was afraid for me, because I'd almost abandoned him, because he had almost been left alone and he didn't know how to deal with the anxiety into which the very thought of that possibility plunged him. It was almost like the times when, instead of hugging me, Leopold would shout at me whenever I went climbing trees and bloodied my nose in the process. It was absurd, this masculine empathy, but it didn't bother me. As long as Maximilian was still angry with me, I knew he could feel. It got worse when he discovered his famous officiousness. After a month or so he stopped reacting to my attempts to talk about my sorrow. It wasn't that he rebutted them, he just failed to hear them. While I was trying to lay out whether it was possible that I was at fault for Anna dying, whether something was wrong with me, or whether my body was actually a killing machine that perhaps ought to be taken out of commission, he insisted on talking about public affairs. Criticizing various people. Reading out loud from the newspaper. It was as though he were talking to the wall. Just one more time he told me:

"Nada, life has to go on. People who cling to their sorrow are emotionally disturbed. Normal people move on."

I didn't want him to think I was emotionally disturbed. I wanted him to respect me, and respect obviously came as a reward for being resilient. I have to be strong, I told myself, and if I'm not strong, I have to at least pretend that I am. So I stopped being insistent with him. And while I was trying to recover in whatever way would be least troublesome for him, he was fucking my chambermaid and gave her a child.

Secretly, I hoped that there was only a limited number of shocking things that could happen to a person in their lifetime, since too many of them would disrupt the pattern of the narrative. Jakob's death, I had to think, had been the last big event of my life and I would need several years to process it before I could be done with it, more or less – and then settle into the kind of boring state that was typical of grown people, and then wait for my life to pass by.

And yet here I was, sitting at this table as though I'd just now been born, as though the world were starting all over from scratch, as though nothing had been completed and everything was still fresh, as though I'd never yet once tried to understand anything, as though I were a child whom someone had just today told for the first time that kitties have to die someday, too.

I don't know what Maximilian felt when he found out about Jakob and me, but what shook me most about the story of Ruslana's child was that I could no longer look at my husband as someone I knew, or even someone about whom I knew anything that was true. Suddenly he just decomposed in front of my eyes into an object that I knew absolutely nothing about. I might as well have been gazing at stars. I looked at him, this person with whom I'd lived for eighteen years, and I had no idea who I was looking at. What he said was so completely different from what he did that I couldn't even understand how he managed to reconcile it all for himself. This person, whom everyone else saw as an exemplar of normalcy, was second to none when it came to sheer madness, including Leopold, who everyone thought was insane, and myself, whom Maximilian treated as a madwoman. That thought might have been a comfort to me, except that it insinuated itself differently, as a bothersome reminder that nothing was as it seemed, and thus would remain forever incomprehensible.

I could have slapped Ruslana if I'd run into her, I could have pulled her hair out by the roots, not so much out of jealousy, as because I couldn't bear the thought of her having bowed and scraped around me with her weepy eyes while I was in mourning, feeling sorry for me, her poor missus, who was aware of nothing and mustn't find anything out, her poor missus, who had always thought she was part of whatever happened around her and would be so hurt if she ever found out that it wasn't like that at all, her missus, who couldn't bear knowing the truth, her missus, whom she had to protect from the world. That's funny, I thought, her betrayal almost hurts more than Maximilian's. I had always thought that she and I were the ones who were bound together by something, but now I saw that she'd had a child with my husband.

"Well," Maximilian said, "what do you think?"

There was nothing to write with at hand. For a while I just looked at Maximilian like the golden fish of fairy-tale fame. Nervous breathing caused my mouth to open at intervals.

"Nada?" he asked. "Are you all right?"

Suddenly I remembered the sign language that Sasha had taught me when I was little. I stretched the three lesser digits of my right hand, from the ring to the little finger, straight upright, with with my thumb and index finger forming a recessive o, to create an "f". Then, as if in counterbalance, the index and ring fingers of my right leapt up as if swearing an odd, English oath, a "u". Next, the ring and index fingers together curled downward to meet my upwardly curling thumb: "c". Finally, my trusty duo of ring and index fingers swept around to show their backs to Maximilian, as my thumb crept up to scowl out through them, which was "k".

"Did you just tell me to fuck off?" Maximilian asked.

I nodded in what was almost elation. Even when we used real words, we had rarely understood each other so well.

22

Although Freud immediately agreed to see me, I spent some time pacing nervously back and forth on the Berggasse, smoking and playing for time. He must be angry at me, he probably assumes the worst, I thought. Will he reproach me? Shout at me? I must have been ten minutes late for my appointment already, and my bad conscience for being late was only intensified by my fear of chastisement.

When he opened the door, I wanted so much to apologize that I almost forgot that I couldn't speak.

"Come on in," he said in a voice that threatened no punishment. "I'll get you a pencil and paper."

I'm sorry, I scrawled on a sheet of paper as soon as we were both seated.

He shook his head and brushed it off, as if to say I have no idea why you think you need to apologize. He wasn't my husband, he wasn't my father, and my insults had been nothing personal for him, they were just something that came with the job, he expected them the way an obstetrician expects to see at least some blood at each birth. But the more dismissive he was of them, the more guilty I felt. Look at this magnanimous person, who doesn't even flinch when you call him a charlatan and accuse him of greed. So of all the people in the world, you had to go and insult him? As though Maximilian and his ilk, and even you, who consider yourself a sensitive person, hadn't already condemned him enough, so you had to let yourself go at him just so you could avoid being in a position that was uncomfortable? Suddenly I saw what I must have looked like to Rachael Frischauer. Spoiled, greedy and full of unbearable self-righteousness.

I really am sorry, I wrote again. *You must know I don't really think that it's just about the money for you.*

"There you go, trying again to avoid talking about yourself by talking about me," he said. Still, I think he welcomed the apology.

He leaned back in his chair, clasped his hands over his stomach and thought for a while. Then, with a dramatic flourish worthy of an operetta, he leaned forward, reached for one of the figurines arrayed on the desk before him, picked it up and turned it towards me. It was a tiny, white monkey with a taciturn face, hands resting on its knees, belly full. This monkey, he's going to say now, I thought to myself, this monkey is you. Whenever Leopold wanted to tell Wanda she was stupid, he almost invariably called her a monkey. Evidently I still expected Freud to reveal sooner or later that he really was angry with me, that he hated me, but was prevented by professionalism from expressing it adequately.

"This," Freud said, "is Toth's baboon."

I examined it far too intensely, as though I meant to show Freud that I wasn't going to disappoint him, as if it meant more than anything in the world to me for him to see me as his diligent pupil, for him to think I was serious. It had a funny face, the little monkey, and yet it looked thoughtful and wily.

It has the same sort of face as you, I wrote on the sheet in front of me.

"You're too kind," Freud said, laughing. "You probably know that Toth gave mankind one of the most precious gifts it has ever received?"

I shrugged. I'd never been much interested in Egyptology.

"Writing," he said. "Toth gave the Egyptians writing."

I nodded. I was waiting for his introduction to develop into something that had to do with me.

"I see you're impatient, so I won't bore you with mythology. What I'm trying to say is that you would do well to rely on that gift."

I can't help but, I wrote.

"Not just because of that. I think you would do well to go somewhere for at least a month and try to write in earnest. Everything you remember, everything that seems important to you, everything that seems inconsequential to you but demands your attention just the same, your dreams, your memories, a running diary, in short, everything that you haven't been able to tell me outright here, even when there was nothing wrong with your voice. I told you about Toth, because I think the ancient Egyptians were right to believe that writing gave mankind mastery over things, and I think it's going to help you regain a sense of control over your own life. Let me suggest, let me say I'm almost positive that before you manage to write just half of what you have to say about your life, you'll start talking again. If that doesn't happen, then at least we'll have something to deal with when you come back. I think it's also going to be useful for you to absent yourself from your usual surroundings. Sometimes it's helpful to be able to look at things from a distance. Seriously now, go on vacation and write, and when you come back to Vienna, let's meet again."

I nodded. It had sounded like sensible advice. I was tired of everything, my body felt heavy and most of the time I felt as though I wasn't going to be able to drag myself out of my dreams in the morning, as though I were caught somewhere halfway between this world and some other, as though my legs were wrapped in thick fog and had to slog through it with great effort, slowly, almost imperceptibly. A change of surroundings could really be helpful.

Instead of going straight home from Berggasse, I stopped by to see Helene. I wanted to offload all of my practical concerns onto her, I wanted her to do the work of survival for me, I wanted her to think where I could go and how much time I could stay there, I wanted her to arrange things with money, arrange things with people, to play the role of the mother I'd never had. My will was too weak for me to do myself up in all the conventional vanities. I wanted to submit myself to another's mercy completely, as though I were crippled and didn't have any choice.

Helene was practically made to take care of me, and I still wonder if I ever showed her clearly enough how much I really owed her. She was unparalleled for the depth of her understanding, Helene was. She didn't condemn Maximilian, he was her brother and she loved him, but even so, without needless prying, she also understood that I couldn't be with him. And of course she knew all the right people.

"Princess von Thurn und Taxis has a wonderful little castle in Duino," she said, "and she loves having visitors, especially if they give her decent fodder for gossip. I'll write to her now. I'm sure she'll love having you there. And besides, she talks so much herself that she won't even notice that you can't."

She paused for a moment.

"While we're waiting to hear back, will you stay here?"

May I? I wrote.

"Of course, for as long as you like. Shall I write to Maximilian, or would you prefer to contact him yourself?"

Would you write to him for me? I wrote.

She simply nodded back and everything was set in motion. The next morning, when Maximilian insisted that he needed to speak to me, through the door of the guest room I could hear her telling him very calmly to go home.

"You both need some time alone," she said.

"What do you know what either of us needs?" I heard him say. After that came the sound of the door slamming.

He came back on the following day. On the day after that he just sent over a suitcase containing my clothes. And then, on the next day, a letter arrived in which the Princess von Thurn und Taxis wrote that she was looking forward to my arrival and that, as far as she was concerned, I could arrive tomorrow and stay for as long as I deemed necessary. By the fifth day I was already sitting aboard an express train headed for Trieste. As I took my seat by the window, I couldn't help but see myself boarding the train for Lemberg to escape the consequences of my own decisions, but soon I realized that, aside from a train that would take me from Vienna to the farthest extremes of the empire, that departure and this one had nothing in common. This time I wasn't leaving *in medias res*, still attached to what I was presumably leaving. This time, although I still hadn't had time to really think it over, I was leaving for good, as though I'd come to the final word of whatever still bound my future to my past in a coherent story, as though I vaguely, but no less finally, sensed that it was time to put the past to an end and start anew. Perhaps it was because I was deprived of speech, but none of these thoughts took shape as a sentence – they came to me in the form of actions that I might be able to explain today, but at the time I was simply reacting, like someone who's starving or bloodied up. I chose the trans-Alpine route, so that I wouldn't have to pass through Graz and Bruck, so I could look out at the tops of the mountains to which I was bound by nothing, which reminded me of nothing, and that's precisely what I did – I didn't try to guess what Maximilian might be thinking at that moment and if he might already be writing to me. I didn't think about that and I couldn't. What was the point of considering those things when I was so cruelly removed from any control over my own life? I stared out the window, at a forest, at some hollows, at the steep slope of a grassy hillside, at the cutout peaks of the Alps, as though sight were the only sense that was still in touch with anything real. They were like a painting, the Alps in the light of the afternoon sun. Even if you knew the whole time that they had to be swarming with detail, that everything in them was alive, that there were worms and bugs with tiny feelers hidden beneath each stone and a fox burrowed and dozing under every root, the eye still presented them as a monumental, unified picture of grey rock flung up against the sky, which, without having to explain anything, without having to work itself up into a storm or an avalanche, by dint of its sheer immensity told you how insignificant you were and how very far removed from everything. It sounds as though the sight of them must have been painful for me, but in fact it was nice. I was alone, and the most I could do for myself was to feel that solitude. At the Trieste station, where I handed my bags to the driver that Princess Thurn von Taxis had sent to meet me and drive me back to Duino, for a moment I felt like dropping everything I had and disappearing into the smell of coffee and salt water that hovered over the pavement. Like walking into the sea. Boarding some ship. Going to work in a brothel. Cutting all of my ties. Instead, I just nodded my thanks and got into the car.

I liked him, this man who had come to fetch me, this man who later turned out not to be the driver, but the castle's custodian, Carlo. He was quiet by nature and you could tell that he wasn't once tempted to engage me in conversation, not because they had warned him beforehand that the mute woman he was being asked to pick up mustn't be put in an awkward position, but because he himself felt no need. I even liked the car, which was closer to nature than I was accustomed to. It didn't lock me inside or protect me from anything. It seemed to be just another part of the road it was driving down. And the seacoast in August, the long, sloping sward that, cut off, dropped into the sea, the golden light falling onto it, summer in decline with Trieste at my back, all of it was appealing. Even the princess herself, who out in the courtyard of her summer residence gave me the kind of ironclad hug that ageing spinsters use to startle their visitors' children, despite her square head and logorrhoea, even she was likeable in her way. It was alien to me, all of this, it shut me out and seemed unreal, like purgatory, like the space between worlds where it was impossible to belong, for which no one can be accountable. I wasn't happy, that August of 1911 in Duino, as I climbed into my temporary bed that was too short. I was profoundly unhappy, but I was where I needed to be, which was nowhere.

23 "Do you know Rilke?" the princess asked me at breakfast one morning. She was reading her mail, and because I'd been staying at Duino for almost four months, I knew that she read it the way Maximilian read the newspaper – as though reading was a public activity that it would be a shame to engage in alone. She took pleasure in reading choice excerpts from her letters to me out loud and with commentary. Sometimes while reading she would burst out laughing, then fall silent and wait a moment for me to ask what was so funny, only then recalling, I suppose, that I couldn't speak, and so she'd go on to explain the matter herself.

I shook my head. I didn't know him. All I knew was that Helene knew him.

"Oh, he's a marvellous poet," she said, "and an absolute angel. I hope the two of you can meet, I'm sure you'd get along marvel-lously. I'm forever inviting him to come join me in Duino, and though each time he acts as though nothing in the world would give him more pleasure, ultimately he never does come to visit. He's just written to me from Paris to say he probably won't be coming this year, either, because the thought of the cholera outbreak in Venice makes him nervous. Sometimes I worry about him so, he's so fragile and so not of this world, I can hardly see how he survives."

Like Helene, the princess also knew everybody who was worth knowing, except that her interest in people resembled a hobby in which one collects broken toys. If I wanted to be mean, I might say that the princess fed on other people's pain, but that would sound cruel, and the princess was anything but. In fact she was caring and kind, but she also seemed determined to surround herself with hopeless cases whom she could worry about forever, whom she could look after forever, comforting and being there for them. No wonder she'd grown so attached to me.

"Do you think I should get in the car and go get him myself?" she asked, as though my opinion were of any importance in deciding this.

I shrugged. I really didn't care.

"Would you be upset? Would it bother you if he joined us?"

What on earth would I have to be upset about? It was her castle and she could invite whoever she wanted to visit her there, and if she wanted, she could haul them over the Alps on her back by the dozen. Asking for my permission was sheer symbolic courtesy. I shook my head.

"Wonderful!" she exclaimed, clapping her hands together. "You'll be here on your own for about a week, but you'll get by, won't you?"

I would have offended her if I'd said that being alone would be a relief, so again I just silently nodded.

"Then it's decided. I'll leave you the other car. Carlo can drive you to Venice anytime, if you want a diversion. I'm going to leave you Rilke's last book, so you can get to know our new housemate. You're going to like him immensely, you'll see," she said once more with conviction.

And indeed, it had been decided. I was left alone at Duino with Carlo, his black greyhound, and the princess's copy of *The Notebooks of Malte Laurids Brigge*, which I was absolutely sure I wasn't going to read.

If I had come to write, you couldn't have told that from the way I behaved. I'd tried a few times, but it refused to take. I acted as though I had a very clear idea, even though I had none, of what I needed to write and what it would look like, something that no reality lived up to. My handwriting was ugly and crude, my thoughts were disorganized, and whenever I tried to write what I felt qualified as "literature", it sounded false, and if I tried to write something that aspired to be "true," it sounded ugly and cruel. There wasn't a single sheet of paper that I burdened with my writing that escaped the flames. Everything I reached for in my efforts to express myself had to be burned, as though it were the rags of a leper that were best destroyed. I had nothing to say. As I climbed up and down over the rocks of the shore, I kept thinking that maybe Ruthenian wasn't the language that I needed to perfect in order for my soul at last to find its expression, perhaps that language was silence, which I spoke and clearly also wrote fluently, without ever having to learn it. As Carlo, his dog and I ate our supper of eggs and cheese in silence, I often thought that this life, which was so monastic, was perhaps the life I'd been fated to live. No matter how much I hated Maximilian when he tried to send me to the asylum, somewhere deep down I thought he was right. Maybe, I thought, some of us really didn't belong in this life.

With the same persistence with which I kept rejecting my own writing, Maximilian's letters arrived. At first he was angry with me. Angry, because I'd left without giving him the chance to defend himself, to talk things out with me and say everything he believed I needed to know or understand. That I'd left as though I had no responsibility to him, as though I were alone in the world, because I was egotistical and unfeeling and had slammed the door in his face. *I'll bet*, he wrote, *that you don't even feel any guilt. You've always had an acute sense of when others needed to feel guilty, of when others ought to behave more responsibly than they were capable of, or at least fall on their knees and beg for forgiveness. Considering how good you are at condemning others, it's almost unbelievable how little guilt and responsibility you feel for your own actions, what aristocratic self-satisfaction you feel about all of your own decisions, and how everything you do is always at least necessary, if not always right.*

He wanted to insult me, because he knew my vanity, the vanity I'd inherited from Leopold, which from some dark chamber of my soul always reminded me that, forever and at all cost, I had to make sure I could think of myself as good and that, even when I was making mistakes, I wasn't doing it maliciously, just out of weakness. He knew me and it was no shot in the dark when he bet on my bad conscience in the hope of getting a rise out of me. If I'd still considered him someone whose point of view I could borrow in order to get a look at myself around corners that were blind even for me, I might have taken the bait, as he hoped. The bad conscience he was hoping to evoke in me would have arrived like an army decked out with flags, in a cloud of dust raised by the hooves of its horses, burying me and cowing me into apologizing. Bowed under its weight, I would have so hoped he would believe my apologies, believe that I'd had no bad intentions, that I would have completely forgotten what I wanted in the first place. I just would have cried and hoped that he'd understand.

Maximilian's only mistake was in assuming that I still cared how he saw me. And it wasn't just the relationship to him that had changed, it was also the distance that had grown up between me and the world, a distance from which it seemed as though I were observing life from a distant shore and that everything it comprised seemed so small, so far away, and so irrelevant. He hadn't offended me. I understood the anger that comes when another rejects any attempt at working together. I understood it because I had felt it myself, had felt it towards him when he refused to hear my sadness, had felt it towards Jakob when he rejected my plans, and without even realizing it, all my life I had felt it toward Leopold, who never really listened to anyone other than himself. I wasn't offended, but I couldn't allow myself to let the anger affect me. It went past me, as though it were aimed at somebody else.

After the anger came the remorse. *I keep thinking,* he wrote to me now, *about catching a train and coming to see you, but I know that would be disrespectful and I don't want to upset the tranquillity you've chosen for yourself. You haven't answered my letters, so I don't know if you're doing any better, I can only imagine that your health has improved and you've left for Venice, where you spend your time in animated conversations with other tourists about inconsequential things, all the while thinking your own thoughts. I would like you to be healthy, to give some thought to all the things you need to think about, and come back to Vienna, but I know that's something you have to decide for yourself and it's not my place to pressure you one way or the other, and perhaps even asking you to consider it would be scarcely acceptable. So I'll wait and do nothing until you give me your permission. I'll still write you now and then, because I can't help but write, because that's the only way I can still imagine that I remain in any sort of contact with you.*

He had never apologized to me for anything, but now over time his letters began ever more clearly to convey his regret. It would have been hard to say what exactly Maximilian regretted, and to this day I couldn't guess if he knew what he'd done wrong, yet his every word testified to the wish for forgiveness that he had initially tried to force out of me. And although now I could also understand what he was experiencing, what I still felt most of all was how little all of it had anything to do with me.

One after the other, Maximilian's letters, whether hurtful, conciliatory, or melancholy, ended up in the fire, along with my failed attempts at keeping the diary I had promised Freud. Although I concede the possibility that I may have been concealing some emotions from myself, I still don't think I wanted revenge or wanted to hurt him. I just wanted to deal with the remains of my former life that I didn't know what to do with any more. Here I'd broken something again, only this time I didn't have to wonder if it was going to grow back together, because it was totally broken forever. From a distance my entire life with him and even the life I'd led on the side seemed so false, everything that I had once considered essential lay in front of me worthless, like a worn-out divan whose moth-eaten fabric reveals its wooden framework. The only thing real was my immediate reality: Carlo eating his bread soaked in water with his wobbly teeth, the steel sky above the Mediterranean Sea, the fish in the fountain inaudibly opening and closing their mouths. Everything else seemed like a ridiculous ghost that I'd had to think up to keep the time separating birth and death from going so slowly. I'd managed to convince myself for a long time that there was something real about it, but now that was over. Was this dry realism what Freud had wanted from me? Even that didn't matter. I'd long since lost any connection to my ability to speak.

I never did get to Venice. The thought of playing the tourist and forcing myself to enjoy all that overblown beauty was as repellent as the thought of experiencing my life as something of inherent value. But I did let Carlo take me with him to Trieste every time he drove there on errands. It came to be understood that I would get in the car each time he took off, that he would drop me off at the Café Flora on the Piazza Grande and then pick me up several hours later, as though I were a bag of grain that got moved from one spot to another, without ever making any comment about it. I didn't do anything in Trieste, I just sat and drank coffee, often with my eyes closed, and let the smells and the sounds waft over me at will. Amid the jumble of languages it was impossible to make out even what people whose language you understood were saying, so you never heard anyone lie. You just heard life running its course without letting itself be troubled much by the cargo getting loaded onto ships and unloaded from them, a streetcar seeming to drive itself, the seagulls screeching or the rain falling, or footsteps clacking their way across cobblestones. Each time Carlo came back to get me, I thought how nice it would be if he could have come a bit later.

24 That December, when the princess's car delivered her slightly crumpled and peevish angelic poet to Duino, I welcomed him with the kind of jubilation that children must feel who have just grown used to being in complete command of the bodies and lives of their mothers, only to find out that soon they're going to get a little brother or sister. He disturbed my peace, Rilke did, his spine racked from the car's endless crawl through Provence, his eyes swollen from the cross-draft. He disturbed my schedule, my solitary suppers with Carlo, and my idleness, which I didn't want anybody observing for so long that they might unmask it as laziness.

They arrived with a great din, the princess and him, amid a cloud of gravel and gossip, as though in the midst of a deep forest an industrial city had sprouted up overnight, with its workers nervously cycling to work in the factories, its capitalists nervously flipping through ledgers, its streetcars nervously running in circles until their nervous passengers got dizzy and sick.

From the balcony I could hear Rilke asking, even before he was shown to his rooms, where he could find the cook, because he didn't want there to be any awkwardness at supper, since he was a vegetarian, and it would be such a nuisance if they had to throw out a roast made especially for him. He was the kind of person who in the course of a single sentence was capable of apologizing at least five times, without giving the slightest impression he was sorry for anything. He was the kind of person who enjoyed saying things like, "I realize it's a bother, but…" He had the thinnest of skins, the most sensitive teeth, a natural inclination to migraines and the most delicate disposition, which could be derailed by the slightest excitement. I envied him the matter-of-factness with which he assumed the role of the weakest one present, and the absence of the least bit of shame that any normal person would have to feel upon making such a show of feeling sorry for himself. I wanted him to disappear back to wherever he'd come from. When we sat down to supper, I had to exert tremendous effort to keep my face from reflecting my unhappiness. I tried to focus on a dreary still life with parrots. How could a composition of three birds against the background of a cloudy sky be so suggestive of death? Was that why the painting counted as a still life, even though it depicted living things? Through the thin layer of these forced thoughts I could hear Rilke slurping the vegetable soup that had been made especially for him. Under the table my knee started to shake slightly, the way Jakob's had done. Did everybody constantly get on his nerves, too?

"Mrs. Moser is a writer, too," the princess suddenly said in a voice that insisted on my participation. "She's just now completing her autobiography, which draws to a large extent on psychoanalysis. She's a friend of Freud's, you know."

Once again, it was as though Leopold were explaining how he'd wrested me out of the claws of some wolf family and made me human, how he'd trained me to speak and walk on two legs. What on earth had Helene served her up with? Or had the princess taken the few facts she knew about my life and on her own interpreted them in the way that she thought evoked the most curiosity? I don't suppose that saying I was just some melancholy madwoman trying to avoid her husband or perhaps her entire life would have sounded particularly glamorous.

"Do you know my friend Lou Salomé?" Rilke asked.

I shook my head.

"She's also quite an enthusiast for psychoanalysis. She's been trying to convince me for quite a while that I should get myself analysed, but I really don't know quite what to think of it all. I've given it quite a bit of thought and it seems more and more to me that if I got myself dissected like that, all the art would dry up, and art is the only thing that still seems like a meaningful activity to me. I couldn't bear it if I suddenly found I understood myself but didn't have anything left to say."

He sounded so limited to me when he talked like that, so idiotic in his conviction that there was something noble about being mal-adapted, that his weakness was a virtue that ought to be cultivated, without which the things that had ultimate value for him would vanish out of his life, and yet – wasn't I myself living proof that he was right, in a way?

"Shall I bring you a pencil and paper?" the princess asked, having divined from the look on my face, I suppose, that I was thinking intensely enough that I might want to say something. "You realize," she said, since apparently she hadn't had time to explain my situation on the long car trip from Paris to Duino, "Mrs. Moser is suffering from hysterical aphonia and can't speak, so we communicate in writing, more or less."

I didn't know that the adjective hysterical went together with aphonia, I would have said if I'd been able, but as it was I just narrowed my eyes in disagreement.

"How unusual," Rilke said, apparently sharing the princess's enthusiasm for things that had flaws. "Would you mind very much if I asked you not to write this evening? I'd like to try to guess what you're thinking."

It turned out not to be just that evening; Rilke's interest in reading my thoughts in his own way persisted to the end of our brief acquaintance. Whenever I tried to pick up a pencil to answer one of his questions, he would raise his hand to shoulder level and, palm turned outward, signal me to stop.

"I know," he continued, "you think such and such, but I have to tell you that..."

I was almost never thinking what he assumed I was.

"I hope you won't mind," the princess said to Rilke, "but when I left for Paris, I gave her my copy of *Malte*, because I knew she was working on her own autobiography, and I thought how you set about describing a life's story might be of interest to her."

"Really?" Rilke asked, actually sounding interested, for once. "Of course I don't mind. Did you enjoy what you read?"

They had driven me into a corner, the princess and Rilke, they had forced me to add my share to the pile of empty chatter we were engaged in.

I nodded, although I'd completely forgotten that I still had that book.

"That's nice to hear," Rilke said, "although I think that book had a horrible effect on me. I feel so empty, as though I scraped everything out of me that was worth anything into that book, and now there's nothing left in me to grab on to."

And yet you think that psychoanalysis is the thing that could destroy you as an artist, I thought, while nodding with restraint.

Before I went to sleep I dug Rilke's book out of a stack of odds and ends where I'd misplaced it. I was more curious than I would have liked to admit, if only because I wanted to prove to myself that I had good reasons for finding our newcomer so hard to take. I couldn't hold out to the end. What he wrote upset me almost more than what he said. It was the story of a human life, that book, and yet there was nothing human about it, it was all so wordy and blurry, it all sank into an art whose main concern was to make everything as unrecognizable and unsolvable as possible, to deepen the shadows and fog and disorder, to not look life in the face, to avoid confronting itself and to flee from any self-knowledge. Suddenly I knew how I needed to start telling the story of my life. The way Rilke would never have done. I grabbed a stack of paper and started to work without even checking if my handwriting and vocabulary were correct.

At breakfast the next morning the princess announced that she would have to leave us on our own for a certain period of time. It was like when she announced that she would have to leave for Paris immediately to get Rilke, except that this time she had to leave for Vienna immediately, since her son was getting divorced.

"You know," she said, and I already knew what was going to come next, "Pasha is such a sensitive boy, he always has been, even as a child he was more sensitive than most and to this day it's hard for him to endure any emotional upset. I worry about him so much, and he has no one in Vienna in whom he can confide – you know how men are around each other, they'd rather hang themselves from a chandelier than bare their unhappiness, in this world a man can only confide in a woman, and if his own wife is the cause of his anguish, then he can thank his stars if his mother is still alive."

The princess had a mission that required immediate action. Not only was there a sad human being out in the world somewhere, that human being was her own son. Who's to say, I thought, if she's going to care for him any more thoroughly than she cares for Rilke and me, or if all of her concern is superficial, aimed not so much at her mission as at the sense of satisfaction that having a mission gives her. She set out before evening and left us to our own devices.

In the days that followed I did everything to avoid contact with my fellow lodger. Whenever he came to ask if I'd like to take a walk along the cliffs with him, I would raise a hand to my forehead in an overly dramatic gesture, faking a headache. Most days I spent in my room, so persistently pretending to feel ill that I actually began to feel a bit sick. I wouldn't leave my rooms until evening, after Rilke had already retired to sleep, with the stealthy step of a burglar making my way down the staircase to take a stroll through the gardens, so I wouldn't forget what the world on the outside looked like. It was a warm December, with bright stars shining over the silent Karst plateau. It's funny, I sometimes thought, this is still Austria, but it feels like I'm at the end of the earth. When I returned to my room I would write, hysterically, imprecisely, out of a need to compete with that person who fancied himself a writer, even though he lacked the courage to say anything real, out of a competitiveness that I found hard to admit even to myself, yet there it was, an inaudible clockworks of my soul proving that all mechanisms that drive a person to action are always at least a little bit spurious.

We lived apart from each other, maintaining the distance between us, until he came gently knocking on my door the morning before Christmas. As though he were waiting for me to answer, he knocked twice, then he must have remembered he was dealing with someone who couldn't speak, and he timidly entered the room.

"Forgive me for bothering you," he said after seeing I was still in bed, and then bashfully looked away, as though he'd caught me naked. "I just wanted to ask if you might like to have supper with me this evening, since it will be Christmas Eve and we see each other so seldom that I sometimes forget I'm not here alone."

I nodded, not least because I also needed some company.

"Splendid!" he exclaimed, clapping his hands together like a small child. "I've had a Christmas tree delivered, and it would please me so much to be able to share it with somebody. Will five o'clock work for you?"

I nodded again and Rilke, head bowed, left my room.

This is my birthday, I suddenly remembered when I got up and started looking through my dresses, today is my thirty-seventh birthday. I'm almost forty and I've achieved nothing. I understand nothing any better than I used to, nothing seems any more certain, or solid, or dependable, just my reflection in the mirror quietly reminded me that signs of wear had begun to show on my body, in my face, in my hair, and that the earth, which in Leopold's words gave birth to me, would sooner or later demand me back. Although I'd never been habituated to beauty, I sometimes enjoyed studying myself. I liked smiling at my reflection and practising a seductive look, I liked finding the angle at which my eyes would look their most mysterious, even if I wasn't thinking about anything particularly deep. But I suddenly realized as I stared at my breasts, which had started to sag, and my hair, which had lost its former gleaming colour, that youthful vanity had been replaced by something else, a kind of grim apprehension that didn't testify to any loss of self-confidence, but rather the terror that comes with the thought of life's transience. I had woken up and there I was, suddenly old. I put on my make-up more carefully than ever before in my life, to keep anyone else from noticing.

I got the idea of taking some time before supper to sort through my notes, to finally have a good look at what had poured out of me in the course of the previous days, and to mark my birthday with a sort of intimate encounter with myself, but everything I had written suddenly struck me as cruel and unfair. What just the evening before I'd seen as something that at least at its core resembled the truth, now revealed itself to be merely the uncontrolled rage of a spoiled child incapable of even imagining there might be anyone else in the world except for himself who thought or felt anything worthwhile. How many people would I have saddened, if what I had written ever became public? I threw the sheaf of pages I was holding into the fire and lay back down. Through the windows I could hear a storm was rising.

We had supper in silence, Rilke seeming like a frightened child who out of fear of his strict governess stifled any needless questions about the nature of the world that he might have wanted to ask in more relaxed circumstances. His nervousness made him clumsy when, after dinner while trying to light the candles on the tree he'd somehow managed to find, he came close to burning the castle to the ground. Thankfully Carlo with a glass of water managed to douse the branch of the tree that caught fire.

I felt sorry for him and sorry that my grimness had ruined the celebration he'd devised. I'd do best to get out of the way, I told myself. Before I left, I put my hand on his shoulder and hoped he would understand how sorry I felt. He looked at me with those calf eyes of his and placed a hand over mine, then I got my coat and headed out into the bora.

The wind was driving tiny snowflakes over the cliffs. Winter, so long delayed, had arrived with a jolt, the weather grown inhospitable, announcing that nature, although it encompassed us, too, was merciless and cruel. Every gust of wind was like a fist in your stomach, a hand slapping your face, every gust of wind announced that violence was the most real expression of existence and everything else at least to some extent fake. In my life I had never known anyone who made a big show of being evil and cruel. I'd only known good people, people who put stock in kindness and empathy, and yet even those people, including myself, had sown nothing but division and unhappiness around them. Even if you'd never spoken out for evil, was there any way to avoid it?

I was already most of the way on the path over the cliffs towards the Bay of Sistiano when the fatigue I'd been feeling those past several months overwhelmed me. I couldn't go forward or back, my legs were moving the way they move in dreams, and my body rejected motion and came to a stop overlooking the sea. Although I'd never known any suicides, until then I'd assumed that suicide was a thing of the intellect, that it accompanied a person like a philosophical discourse for months, maybe years, that it was the result of carefully calculated considerations or at the very least a badly calculated effort at blackmail, but suddenly it appeared it was neither of those things. It didn't belong to the domain of reason or even the domain of emotion, it was the body's decision, borne out of darkness, to opt for rest rather than motion. I didn't want to jump off the cliff, I just leaned out over it, as though my body wanted to fall off of its own accord.

Although lightning is extremely rare in a snowstorm, I have never been tempted to view it as an intervention of fate. It was just lightning in a snowstorm, a flash in the darkness and the sound of a thunderbolt to which I responded with uncomplicated, childlike fear, jumping back from the edge of the cliff onto the trail, where I landed awkwardly, tearing my dress and falling on my arse. Were you, a voice deep inside me said, just a moment ago about to throw yourself off the cliff, and now you're jumping back in fear of death? With no awareness of starting, all of a sudden I was laughing at the top of my voice amid the gravel and snow. Something that had broken had just now grown back together.

I ran all the way back. On the road up to the entrance I ran into Carlo, who looked like he was discreetly trying to determine where I might have disappeared to.

"Carlo, drive me to Trieste," I said.

He didn't bat an eye at the sound of my voice, he just opened the door on the passenger's side, climbed in behind the wheel, and off we drove.

25 "Just as long as you don't think," Emilie said to me when I came to pick up the dress she had sewn for me, "that getting rid of your corset all by itself means that you're liberated."

"Don't worry about me," I said laughing. 'It's been ages since I was naive enough to expect easy solutions from life."

"People often think that they've shed their naiveté, but then they still get an unpleasant surprise."

I looked at her and said, "How I wish I could think you're not right, Emilie."

"You think I don't?"

We hugged and I left. I'd been back in Vienna for a week and it was time for me to meet Maximilian.

He welcomed me like an honoured guest. He was stiff and formal, which meant he was afraid.

"Would you like coffee?" he asked me stupidly as we sat down, each at his own end of the dining-room table, as though we were settling business matters.

I shook my head: no. I had no interest in coffee, all I wanted was for this Calvary to attain some kind of epilogue. Because I've never had any of my own money, it's hard for me to guess how people must feel who've spent decades of their lives under the heavy burden of debts, but I doubt they feel very different to how I did. I bore the weight of the past, the only thing I still wanted in life was to unburden myself of it.

"I don't want any coffee, Maximilian, I want a divorce."

Maximilian leaned back in his chair, but only with half of his back and his right shoulder, with his left shoulder still leaning greedily forward, the elbow bent, the left hand, with fingers pointing towards the inner side of the knee, resting on his thigh. It was a practised pose that announced a practised speech was to follow. He was prepared.

"Yes, I've noticed that that ridiculous mother of yours wrote in her memoirs that the option of divorcing is the sole condition for a woman to be happy."

I'd heard that Wanda had published her memoirs, but I didn't dare read them. Did she write that her own daughter left her to starve, with no roof over her head?

"You didn't know her, Maximilian, and you have no right to say she's ridiculous. And no, it's not because of something Wanda wrote that I want a divorce, and it's not even because of you. It's for my-self that I want a divorce."

"Isn't the reason people get married precisely in order not to keep thinking only about themselves?"

"Oh, come on, Maximilian. You know that's not true."

"Even your late socialist boyfriend could have told you that individualism poisons happiness."

"Don't bring Jakob into this, please. Don't stoop so low."

In order to achieve his goal, Maximilian must have thought that all available means were admissible. And he wasn't inclined to be diplomatic. Clearly, any sense of guilt had left him the very instant he saw me, and he began to construe my return as the prologue to his victory. He was inclined to be cruel.

"What do you mean, stoop so low? It simply seemed to me that even you, perhaps even more than I, ought to understand that sometimes a person has to sacrifice his pride, if it means serving the greater good."

"What greater good, Maximilian? What good can possibly come from forcing ourselves to live together?"

"And what do you propose to live off of as a divorced woman, if I may ask?" Maximilian asked, even before anyone said that he might. When you don't want to reply to a question with an answer, he must have thought, answer it with another question. It was very stupid of me to try to answer it.

"I thought that I might be able to support myself by writing," I said.

He laughed, loudly.

"Who are you kidding?" he said after the laughter died down. "It's all very well to have an imagination, but do you have any idea what style of life you're accustomed to and what style you'd be forced into if some third-class newspaper did publish a couple of your stories per year? If they published them at all, that is? Have you even published anything before in your life, or did you just assume that sort of talent is inherited? And even if it were, you know you're not really related to Sacher-Masoch or to that ridiculous mother of yours."

It had been really, really very stupid of me to answer his question. I had wanted not to have to cry, but the wish was weaker than the impulse. He had done me a favour with his cruelty, Maximilian had. Before I arrived, I had been prepared not to be able to leave him, prepared for his face and voice to remind me that what one has grown accustomed to is always hard to leave behind, even if you have good reasons for doing so; that the house in which I'd lived for so long without ever really becoming fond of it would suddenly seem like my home, that it would fill me with doubt and delay. But Maximilian's fury and the humiliation that accompanied it made any hesitation impossible.

"One more time, I ask you," I said in a voice that was spoiled by sobbing, "please stop insulting Wanda. You didn't know her, you don't have any right."

"But I'm not insulting her, dear heart, you yourself said that she had to sew gloves to survive, and went to look at the bread in the bakeries so she could at least imagine eating it, until Sacher-Moser rescued her."

"If you call that rescuing."

"Well, what would you call it? Would it have been better for her to die of malnutrition?"

'Perhaps, Maximilian," I said, even though I surely didn't believe it. "Perhaps it would have been better if she'd died of malnutrition."

"You can't possibly mean that."

"I know that I think it's better to be on one's own than unhappy."

"How many times have you been on your own, if I may ask?"

"Have you noticed that each time you ask your question first, and then ask for permission?"

"Don't answer a question with another question, Nada."

"You're right, you're the only one allowed to do that."

"Do you know what I think?" he suddenly asked.

"No, Maximilian, how should I know that?"

"That you have a new lover."

"Oh, please, Maximilian, is it so hard for you to imagine that I might want to leave you because of you?"

Suddenly I had become cruel, myself. It happened spontaneously, and it came too naturally for me to resist.

"No, really," he said. "I don't believe you would leave me if another man weren't already involved. You don't know how to be alone, you'd go crazy. I think you've fallen in love with that Rilke fellow from Duino."

"Have you been spying on me?"

"So I was right."

"I think this conversation is over."

I got up to leave, but if I wanted to reach the door, I had to walk the length of the table, and before I got halfway, Maximilian was blocking my path. All of his manners had vanished – God knows where. With his right hand he grabbed me by the hair at the nape of my neck. You're stronger than I remember, I thought.

"I knew I was right."

"Maximilian, please, let me go," I said with feigned calm in my voice.

"Or else, what will happen?"

He threw me onto the table as if he were tossing a log on the fire. I landed face-first on the tea service and lace tablecloth, and while his left hand took hold of me by the neck, his right hand unbuttoned his trousers. You have no right to walk out whenever you feel like it, he must have been thinking. But had he noticed how readily he gave himself the right to detain me whenever he felt like it? I could say that I came to hate him at that very moment; I almost wish I could say without hesitation that I started to hate him at that moment, but in fact something far more complicated took place. I felt as though he were finally giving me a chance at an honest fight, as though he'd finally revealed himself to be what he must have been all along, as though he were finally giving me permission to see the monster hiding behind the fastidiously combed moustache, the flawless jacket, and engage with it in the way it deserved – monstrously.

I propped myself up by my wrists until my face was level with his. Hm, I'm stronger than I remember, too, I thought. I lunged at him, knocking him onto the floor. Anyone who has seen two dogs playing can picture with considerable clarity how far removed our panting was from love.

"I'm sorry," Maximilian said when it was over. He was sad.

"So am I." But I wasn't sad, I was amazed.

"So you still want to get divorced, do you?"

I nodded.

"Why?"

"Because living a lie makes me more unhappy than living alone and in poverty."

"I still think you can say that only because you've never known either poverty or loneliness."

"I know you still think that."

"How about," he said with the voice of someone who wants to make a suggestion, "if we agree to this: you can move to Trieste and we never have to live together under the same roof again. Just let me pay you a modest allowance and we'll have dinner together once a year."

"You'd rather bribe me for the rest of your life than officially divorce?"

"That's right."

"And what would that give you?"

"I don't know."

"Maybe you're the one who couldn't endure being lonely."

"Could be."

I kissed him on the nose. I knew that if I were to accept his offer, I would still feel indebted to him, perhaps even more so, but I couldn't endure it, either. Breaking the tie was just so hard.

"All right," I agreed.

He nodded and gave me a hug as we lay amid broken teacups and ripped clothes on the dining-room floor.

26 "You can flee to the ends of the earth, if you want," Freud said when I came to bid him farewell, "but you can't escape from yourself."

"And yet," I said, "you have a right to choose a home for yourself that doesn't remind you day after day you're a misfit."

"Be sure to write me when you find it," he said, laughing. "Maybe I'll come and join you."

I reached out my hand. He didn't take it, but bent over it to give me a hug. A gripping, relentless, full-body hug, a symptom, he himself might have said if he'd been able to see himself from the outside, that in view of its strength had to be rooted in several causes. And here was Freud, engulfed in this embrace, so utterly fragile in this unaccustomed nearness, a dam whose essence was to constantly oppose the water, always on the verge of collapsing. Everything that had never been manifested in his words or even his gestures, lay revealed in his scent, which had only now become accessible in the unforeseen, almost inappropriate nearness of this hug. Freud's was that meticulous, choice scent that seemed to be imperceptible but was consistent in its mission to protect his vulnerability from the assaults of a prying world, and from the taut, contradictory truth beneath it, the sour smell of efforts to staunch physical decline, to limit and deliberately civilize the desires that implacably pull at the body, each in its own direction: exertion, sweat, nicotine, ageing.

But he didn't break. And he didn't give me his blessing.

I knew he was right, and yet sitting outside the Stella Polare drinking champagne was so much like freedom that I might nearly have forgotten about that here, at the end of the earth.

"I knew you'd come back!" a familiar voice exclaimed, followed by a rubbery body and a face with a thin smile. "Where are you staying?"

"In the Savoy Excelsior," I said.

"Oh, splendid! Are you going to become one of those people who live in hotels?"

"Maybe. It might really suit me, don't you think?"

"Like a glove," he said.

I didn't really know him, this person. But on Christmas Eve, when Carlo drove me soaking and shaking into Trieste, he had been the first drunk I had a chance to practise my newfound speech with.

"Will you join me over here, miss? You seem so lonely," he had said in his odd German when I came in.

"How did you know I'm not Italian?" I had asked.

"You look too sad."

Poor Italian girls, I thought. Clearly they're not allowed to show when they're sad.

"Poor Italian girls. Clearly they're not allowed to show when they're sad."

I felt seized by a sort of exhausted hilarity, as if after a night on the town. I didn't have enough strength to maintain any kind of a pose. My hairdo was coming apart and it didn't make sense to try fixing it now.

"You're not from around here, either," I said.

"Of course I am."

"All right, fine, but you haven't always been. Where are you from?"

"I'd rather not say. And you?"

"Oh, I'd be happy to tell you, but I don't know if I know."

This sudden sense of ease, I thought, had it come with the approach of this stranger or of death? How nice it was to be able to speak without any feeling that somewhere there was a printed script you had to follow.

"You're so pretty," he said as his right hand needlessly smoothed back a lock of hair.

"Please," I said and took hold of his hand, which remained suspended in the air over my ear. "Wouldn't you rather the two of us just get drunk?"

"Don't you believe in love?" he asked in an exaggeratedly mocking tone.

"My father liked to say that love between a man and a woman won't be possible until women are allowed to live on the same terms as men."

"Your father was a wise man."

"He certainly thought so, yes. Let's just say he was a better theoretician than a practitioner."

"What about you?"

"Oh, I'm probably the worst practitioner I've ever known."

"You were practically made for living in Trieste," he said.

"Do you really think so?"

"I can see that you are. Every person who doesn't know what to do with himself eventually winds up in Trieste."

"And here they find out?"

"No, of course not, but at least they can live alongside others like them."

At that moment a woman pushed her way in through the door. She was soaked through like me, pushed her way to the table where the stranger and I were sitting, and began shouting at him in English.

"Dear Jesus, James, it's Christmas and Lucia is sick, I've been looking for you for two hours but you were nowhere to be found. For God's sake come home with me now!"

"Is it really necessary to bring Jesus into everything?" he said as if cracking a joke and gave me a conspiratorial smile.

I'd seen all of it before. All the chaos, all the lack of responsibility, all the people behaving towards each other like bulls in china shops. It was awful, and yet it also suddenly seemed funny. Maybe because it didn't involve me.

"I see you're also a better theoretician than practitioner," I said.

"Oh, I'm even terrible at theory," he said as he got up from the table, following the woman who by all appearances was not amused.

"I'm certain," he said when they were almost out in the street, "this isn't the last we'll see of each other."

"Well," he said to me now, "didn't I tell you we'd see each other again?"

I closed my eyes and nodded.

As Freud said, you can flee to the ends of the earth, you just can't escape from yourself.

THE AUTHOR

KATJA PERAT is a graduate of Philosophy and Comparative Literature and one of the leading poetic voices of her generation in Slovenia. Her first poetry collection *The Best Have Fallen* (*Najboljši so padli*) came out in 2011 and received both the Best Debut Award and the Kritiško sito Award, an award bestowed by the Slovenian Literary Critics' Association for best book of the year. Her second book of poetry *Value-Added Tax* (*Davek na dodano vrednost*, 2014) was also extremely well received. Currently she is a doctoral student of comparative literature at Washington University in St. Louis, USA. *The Masochist* (*Mazohistka*), published in Slovene in May 2018, is her first novel.

THE TRANSLATOR

MICHAEL BIGGINS is responsible as translator for some of the classics of twentieth-century Slovenian literature published in English, including Slovenia's internationally best-selling novel of all time, Vladimir Bartol's *Alamut* (Scala House 2004, reissued by North Atlantic 2007), Triestine-Slovenian author Boris Pahor's memoir of survival in Nazi concentration camps, *Necropolis*, (Harcourt 1995, reissued by Dalkey Archive in 2010), the three-volume auto-fictional novel *Newcomers* by Lojze Kovačič (Archipelago 2016-2020), Drago Jančar's epic tale of plague, religious persecution and survival in late medieval Europe *The Galley Slave*, (Dalkey Archive 2011), *The Errors of Young Tjaž* by Austrian Carinthian Slovene novelist Florjan Lipuš (Dalkey Archive 2013), several collections of poetry by Tomaž Šalamun, and a number of other books. President of the international Society for Slovene Studies since 2017, he lives in Seattle and teaches Slovenian language and literature, as well as Slavic to English literary translation at the University of Washington, where his primary employment is as curator of the university library's growing collection of over a half million volumes in more than twenty languages published across the spectrum of Russian, Baltic, East Central and Southeast European area studies.

CPSIA information can be obtained
at www.ICGtesting.com
Printed in the USA
LVHW011603180121
676807LV00005B/1047

9 781912 545179